Fragile
HEARTS

AMBER KELLY

Cover Design: Sommer Stein, Perfect Pear Creative Covers
Cover Image: Michaela Mangum, Michaela Mangum Photography
Editor: Jovana Shirley, Unforeseen Editing, www.unforeseenediting.com
Proofreader: Judy Zweifel, Judy's Proofreading
Formatter: Champagne Book Design

To my real-life Sonia, who has always deserved more.

Fragile HEARTS

Prologue

BELLAMY
Twelve Years Old

"COME ON. PICK UP THE PACE, YOU GUYS. IT WILL BE DARK soon, and we're going to be in trouble," I yell back to my two best friends, Sonia and Elle, as we race our bikes down the gravel road.

"If I pedal any faster, my legs are going to fly off," Elle pants from the back of the line.

We're on our way back to my house from an afternoon of swimming down at Balsam Cove, and we lost track of time. Momma's going to be fit to be tied by the time we make it to the ranch.

"Bells, we're going to have to stop for a minute. I can't breathe," Sonia huffs, and I look back to see they are both off their bikes and walking.

I slow my pace and pull over to the side of the road. I hop off and wait for them to catch up to me.

"I'm so out of shape," Sonia whines as they finally make it to me.

"Me too. My side hurts," Elle agrees.

"Y'all need to try out for the middle school cheerleading squad with me this year. I promise, Mrs. McGraw would have you two whipped into shape in no time," I encourage them.

"I'm not coordinated enough for cheerleading. Besides, you're the only girl on that squad that I can stand to be around. They're all so snotty," Elle protests.

"Yeah, I'd rather be fat than have to spend every afternoon with the mean girls," Sonia agrees.

"I know they can be uppity, but I wouldn't let anyone treat you guys badly. You know that. And for the record, neither of you are fat. You're a perfect athletic build. That's why I think you should try out. You two would put those girls to shame," I insist.

As we walk along, pushing our bikes, the sound of not-too-distant thunder rumbles beyond the woods.

"Uh-oh, did you guys hear that?" I ask.

We look up and see the rapidly moving black clouds blowing in on the evening breeze. Then, suddenly, lightning strikes across the top of the tree.

We all let out a scream as huge, cold raindrops begin to pound down on us. We drop our bikes in the grass and flee in search of cover. I reach a heavy iron gate at the end of Mashstomp Road and force it open. They follow me as I make my way up the overgrown path that leads to a huge white house that was obviously abandoned long ago. We run to the covered front porch and climb the four steps to huddle under the shelter.

"What is this place?" Sonia asks as she peers into one of the floor-to-ceiling windows that frame each side of the doors.

"It's the Sugarman Homestead. A mansion built by one of the founders of Poplar Falls," I tell her.

"Really? I didn't even know anything was back here."

"That's what Pop told me."

"Does anyone live here?" Elle asks as she joins Sonia at the window.

"I don't think so. Not anymore," I answer as I come up behind them and take a look inside.

"Wow, it's huge! Like, three times the size of our house," Elle says.

"The whole town could live in there," Sonia agrees.

It's not that big, but it is impressive and reminds me of an old Southern plantation, like Tara from *Gone with the Wind*.

"Let's look around back," Sonia suggests and hops off the left side of the porch.

"What about the rain?" I complain.

I'm not a fan of storms. Lightning scares the devil out of me; it has ever since I was little and saw it strike one of the scarecrows in my grandma's garden. He went up in flames and caught her entire field on fire. It happened so fast there was nothing Grandpa could do to stop it.

"Oh, come on. It's just a little rain now. You won't melt. We have our bathing suits on under our shorts," she calls from the side, where she is now climbing the fence.

"What if we get into trouble? The sign says, *No trespassing*," Elle whispers as we make it to the fence and watch as Sonia hops over it and drops to the other side.

"Like the sheriff is going to be out in this weather," she says as she rolls her eyes.

She walks off into the yard at the back of the house. Elle and I are still standing in indecision when she calls to us, "Guys, you have to see this!"

Curiosity finally gets the best of us, and we climb to join her.

Once we make it inside, we follow her path and walk straight into the most beautiful garden we've ever seen. Rose bushes of every color, taller than we are, line a stone pathway that winds through a rainbow of brilliant, fragrant flowers. They go on and on, as far as the eye can see. In the center is a bone-dry stone fountain with three carved cherub angels embracing and laughing.

We take off running through the flower beds, and Elle picks a handful of blooms.

"This place is like the Land of Oz," Sonia muses.

"We need jobs," I declare.

"Jobs? What for?" Elle asks.

"Yes, jobs. If we all get one and start saving our money now, we will have enough saved up to buy this house together when we are, like, twenty years old. We can get married in a three-way ceremony in this garden," I explain.

"Oh, we should marry brothers. That way, we could be real sisters, and our babies will be cousins," Sonia adds.

"Yep, they can be best friends forever, just like us, and we will all live here together, happily ever after!" I agree.

"Let's do it! I bet Gram has chores I can do," Elle exclaims.

"Bellamy!" My brother, Myer's voice comes booming from off in the distance.

We hurry back to the fence and climb over as quickly as we can. Then, we run back toward the gate just as he and his friend Payne Henderson appear.

"Thank goodness," Myer says as he catches sight of us. "Momma got worried about you girls when the storm hit, and she sent us to look for you. We've been searching everywhere. Come on. We already loaded your bikes on the truck. Let's get you girls home," he says as he leads us back to the road.

I look back at the house one more time. *What a treasure.* I hope no one else finds it and we save enough money to buy it one day.

One

BELLAMY
College Graduation Day

"**I** HATE THAT I CAN'T BE THERE, SIS."

I press the Speaker button and place the phone on my bed as I continue to dress for the convocation ceremony. I'm finally graduating from the University of Chicago with a double major in environmental and animal sciences, and I can't wait to get out of here. Don't get me wrong; Chicago is an amazing city, but the winters are brutal, and I'm homesick.

It's funny; when I graduated high school, I couldn't wait to get out of Colorado, but I miss my friends, and now that my brother and his new wife, Dallas, are making me an auntie, there is nowhere I'd rather be at the moment than in Poplar Falls with my family.

"It's okay, Myer. I understand. I'm just hoping my niece or nephew waits at least a few more days before making their grand entrance into the world, so I can be there too," I reassure him.

"Yeah, I'm torn. Momma commanded that he or she stay put as she kissed Dallas's stomach at the airport because she doesn't want to miss the birth of her second grandchild, but Dallas has reached that miserable state of pregnancy, where she can't get comfortable and isn't sleeping at all. She wants to have this baby—like, yesterday— and Beau is about to burst at the seams," he says, and I can hear the chuckle in his voice.

Beau is the cutest seven-year-old boy on the planet. He is Dallas's son from her first marriage, but Myer adopted him last year, and he is very much ours. All of ours.

"Well, that's three of us—if you count Pop—against two. So, hopefully, that little rascal will hold on for us," I say as I pull my long blonde locks into a low ponytail and place my cap on my head.

A loud knock comes at the door.

"Speaking of, I think that's Momma and Pop now, coming to pick me and Derrick up to take us to the main quad. Elle and Sonia are meeting us there," I inform him as I scoop the phone up and grab my purse and keys.

Derrick Chilton is a grad student that I have been seeing on and off for the past couple years. Elowyn "Elle" Young and Sonia Pickens are my best friends. We have known each other our entire lives, and they are like my sisters. They came up with my parents from Poplar Falls for graduation. We have never missed a single important moment in each other's lives. Elle and I were bridesmaids when Sonia married her husband, Ricky, at the end of last year, and both Sonia and I will be bridesmaids when Elle and her fiancé, Walker Reid, get married next year.

"Okay, congratulations, Bells. I'm so proud of you," Myer chokes out.

"Thank you, big brother. Take care of Dallas, and I'll see you guys soon. I love you."

I press the button to disconnect the call and drop the phone in my bag and toss it over my shoulder. I take one last look at myself in the mirror and open the door.

Derrick is standing with my parents, looking dapper in his charcoal-gray suit.

He was a teaching assistant in my biochemistry class. We met my second year at the university and have been dating casually ever since. However, things began to get more serious between us the last few months. He will complete his master's this summer, and he has accepted the position of urban planner at the Columbus Zoo and Aquarium, near his family's home in Powell, Ohio. He has been trying relentlessly to talk me into applying at Columbus as well, but I'm not at all excited by the thought of moving that far from home. Besides, the only available position there is an intern in the planner's office, and the last thing I want is to be working for my boyfriend even if the job is guaranteed and would look good on my résumé. That sounds like trouble waiting to happen.

I did, however, apply for an animal nutritionist position at the Denver Zoo, which is opening at the end of August, and I am anxiously awaiting word back from the department head.

Momma bursts into tears when her eyes hit me in my robe and cap as I wrap my honor cords around my neck.

"Oh, Beverly, don't start blubbering already." Pop rolls his eyes at me and lets out an exasperated sigh before he leans in and kisses my cheek.

"Hush, Winston. It's not like our baby girl graduates from college every day," she says as she swats him out of her way and wraps me in a tight hug. "I'm so proud of you, sweetheart," she whispers into my ear, and a shiver of pride slides down my spine as she releases me and wipes gently at her eyes.

"Don't make me cry and mess up my makeup, Momma. There are going to be a lot of pictures taken today," I grumble as I close and lock the door to my apartment.

Derrick takes my bag from my shoulder and offers me his arm. I take it, and the four of us head down to Pop's rental car to drive us to campus and into my future.

After the ceremony, the six of us head to the Reliance Building in downtown Chicago where we rented the Burnham Room at Atwood with a few other graduates and their families to celebrate. Tonight, Derrick and I are taking Elle and Sonia to see Navy Pier and out on the town. Then, tomorrow, we'll head back to Poplar Falls while Derrick stays on to finish up his program. If all goes according to plan, he will meet me in Denver at the end of the summer and spend a few weeks with me before he heads to his new job. I'm not exactly sure where we will go from there, but we'll figure it out.

"So, what's the plan?" Sonia asks once we order and our cocktails are set in front of us.

"The plan?" I ask.

"Yeah, are you coming home to stay just for the summer, or what?"

I look around at their expectant faces. I haven't had the opportunity to tell them about the move to Denver yet.

"For the summer—for now anyway. I applied for a job at the Denver Zoo, and I'm waiting to hear back from them. It starts at the end of August. I really hope I get it. It's in my field of study, and I would get to work up close and personal with the animals. The pay is good, and I'll only be a day's ride from all of you guys," I tell them.

"I spoke with Dr. Singh there this morning," Derrick interrupts.

I turn to him. "You did?"

This is great news. I put both my biochemistry professor and Derrick down as references on my application. It must mean that they are seriously considering me.

"I did. He said that they have narrowed the selection down to four applicants, and you're still in the running," he assures me.

"Oh, Bellamy, that's wonderful! I'll say an extra prayer that you get the job," Momma squeals.

She definitely prefers that I land in Denver rather than all the way in Ohio. Built-in job or not.

"I sure hope you talked me up, mister," I tease him as I lay a kiss on his lips.

"I did my best," he says on a smile.

"A toast!" Elle announces as she taps her fork against her glass and then hoists it in the air.

"To our bestie, Bellamy's future and one heck of a summer of celebration ahead of us before she runs off to her big-girl job in the city and leaves us all behind again!"

"As if I would ever leave you guys behind. You're stuck with me forever, bitches," I exclaim.

I slide my eyes to my mother as she gives me a stern look.

"Sorry, Momma," I apologize.

"To Bellamy!" Sonia singsongs, and we all clink our glasses.

I'm so happy in this moment. Everything I have dreamed of and worked for is within my grasp.

Once we finish eating and we get my parents settled in at my apartment for the night, the four of us head out to paint the town red.

We start at Navy Pier and work our way back into the city, down the Magnificent Mile, and Derrick ushers us into a horse-drawn-carriage ride.

"Look at you, a lucky man with three beautiful dates this evening," our coachman, Lewis, boasts as he helps us up into our seat.

"Yes, sir, I sure am," Derrick agrees as he settles in beside me and wraps his arm around my shoulders.

Elle and Sonia sit opposite us, and Lewis takes us on a lovely ride while giving us a detailed history behind every building in downtown Chicago.

"Come on. Get in here, so I can take our picture with Coco."

The three of us lean in, so Elle can snap a selfie of us with the horse while Derrick tips Lewis.

She shoots the photo off to Walker via text, and he sends back one of himself and Silas—another employee on Elle's family's ranch—out in their barn with a large black stallion.

His text reads, *That's not a horse, woman. This is a horse.*

"That's Huckleberry. He's a mean ole thing," Elle tells Derrick as she shows off the photo.

We end our evening in a martini bar on State Street with a few of my and Derrick's friends from school.

"Hello?" Sonia is holding her finger in one ear and trying to hear her husband over the phone.

"It's no use," I say as I pop the olive from my glass into my mouth. "You're never going to hear him in here."

"Hold on, baby," she yells into the phone. Then, she points to the door that leads out onto the street and mouths, *I'll be right back.*

She stumbles that direction, and Derrick stands.

"I'm going to follow her. I don't feel good about her wandering off alone," he says before kissing me and following Sonia.

"Aw, I like him," Elle announces as we watch him catch up to Sonia and open the door for her.

"He's sweet," I agree.

"Are you guys exclusive now?" she asks.

I told the girls about Derrick earlier this year, but it was still very casual at the time.

I shrug. "We haven't talked about it, but we've definitely gotten closer this last semester. I guess we'll just have to see how things work out this summer and go from there."

"He's a handsome devil. I like his teeth," she points out.

"His teeth? I think you've had enough," I say as I slide her martini glass away from her.

Derrick and Sonia rejoin us ten minutes later, and she plops down in the stool beside me.

"Everything okay?" I ask as she downs Elle's confiscated drink.

"Just dandy," she says as she wipes her mouth.

I raise my eyebrows at her—the universal girlfriend signal for *spill*—and she sighs.

"Ricky was trying to make me feel guilty for being out, partying, while he is stuck at home, alone."

"Ignore him. Your best friend graduates from college only once. He'll get over it."

"I know," she says, but I can tell her mood has been ruined.

"I know what you need. A pie!" I declare.

"Pie?"

"Deep dish!" Derrick and his buddies yell in unison.

So, we finish our night at Pizano's.

The perfect ending to the perfect day with my favorite people.

Two

Two Weeks Later

"THANK YOU FOR PICKING US UP. MYER REFUSES TO LET ME drive right now," Dallas says as she waddles down the porch steps.

Beau has her hand and is carefully guiding her down to the driveway.

"It's no problem. Are you sure you feel up to this?" I ask.

She looks like she is about to pop at any second.

"Yes, ma'am. I couldn't sit in that house for another minute. Nesting kicked in over a week ago, and I have cleaned out every single closet and drawer and rearranged the furniture in all the rooms. I'm going stir-crazy. Besides, I can't miss Sophie's shower," she says as she hands me the wrapped box she is carrying.

Sophia Lancaster Young is Dallas's best friend, who happens to also be expecting. She is married to Elle's brother, Braxton, and their bundle of joy is due in a few months in the fall. Her mother came into town this weekend to throw her the baby shower to end all baby showers. Elle called me last night and said that four trucks had pulled up to Rustic Peak—the ranch where she lives with her aunts and uncle—loaded down with party supplies.

I place the box into the trunk of my 1966 cherry-red Mustang. It was a graduation gift from Momma and Pop. I've always loved muscle cars, and Pop had this beauty up on blocks under a tarp in the old barn for at least two decades. It was his dad's car, and he had been in the process of restoring it to its original glory when he passed away. While I was in Chicago, Pop had it moved to Jackie's Garage in town, and he and Jackie spent the last couple of years finishing it for me. I love it.

"Can we take the top down?" Beau asks as he climbs into the backseat.

"If it's okay with your momma," I answer.

"Please, Mommy?" he begs Dallas.

"Sure. I'm already sweating like a sinner in church. My hair is going up in a messy knot anyway." She gives in as she plops down in the passenger seat next to me and shuts the door.

I lower the convertible top, and we take off down the road as Beau throws his arms in the air and giggles.

We pull up to Rustic Peak and are assaulted by a barrage of pink. Pink, white, and soft-gray balloons line the long driveway to the house. A large dark wood arch—woven with gorgeous pink, white, and sage-green-colored peonies—stands to the side of the house, leading guests into the backyard.

"Wow, this is something else," I say as I move into the parking spot indicated by the attendant.

"Vivian has outdone herself," Dallas muses as she shakes her head.

Sophie's mother tends to be *extra* in all things. She is a New York socialite, and she forgets—or rather ignores—the fact that Poplar Falls doesn't really do extravagant.

Momma and I along with Dallas's mom—Dottie Henderson—threw Dallas's baby shower in town. Dottie and Dallas own Bountiful Harvest Bread Company and they had purchased the space beside their bakery in January and expanded it to include a small café, where they serve breakfast and lunch sandwiches. We had the celebration there after hours one Saturday evening. Our mothers did all the cooking, and my girls and I decorated in neutral buttercup yellow and brown because Dallas and Myer had decided not to find out the sex of the baby and just to be surprised when the time came.

It was simple and sweet, just what Dallas had wanted, which is the exact opposite of what we see when we round the house and walk through the flowery arch.

"Is that a pony, Mommy?" Beau excitedly asks as I lead him by the hand into what can only be described as a princess garden party.

Pink Chinese lanterns, softly glowing in the twilight sky, are strung on the trees. Underneath the trees are large tables, each one topped with a white tablecloth, a breathtaking centerpiece, and silver candlesticks along with white china and crystal wineglasses, and the chairs are covered in what looks to be pink silk. It's magical.

"Yeah, it sure looks like one," Dallas tells him.

He tugs his hand free of mine and races in the direction of the snow-white pony, wearing a huge pink bow around its neck.

"She bought a newborn baby a pony?" I ask in disbelief.

"Not a newborn. A not-yet-born baby," Dallas points out.

A waiter walks past us with a tray and offers us a glass of pink champagne. I take a flute, and Dallas eyes the tray as she balances our gift on her huge belly.

"Really?" she asks him.

He meets her glare and scurries off.

We hear, "He probably thinks you're just fat," followed by laughter as Charlotte—Sophie's friend and business partner from New York—comes sidling up next to us.

Dallas's glare moves to her.

"Uh-oh, someone is testy," Charlotte surmises.

"No, someone is a hundred months pregnant, and her feet and ankles are the size of watermelons," Dallas whines.

"Well, come on, grumpy momma. Let's get you off those swollen melons and get you something to eat," Charlotte says as she takes the gift from Dallas and steers us to the table where Sophie is seated between her mother and Elle.

"I hate you," Dallas says in Sophie's direction as she drops awkwardly into the seat.

"Hate me? Why?" Sophie asks with her eyes wide.

"Because you look all cute and chipper. And that dress looks great on you. If it wasn't for the fact that it looks like you shoved a little basketball up under it, no one would ever know you were pregnant. I look like I'm wearing a freaking tent, and I had to come in my slippers because none of my shoes fit right now."

"You do not look like you're wearing a tent, Dal. You look adorable," Sophie replies.

Dallas just rolls her eyes at her.

We are served a delicious dinner before Sophie begins opening the insane amount of gifts. Half of which her mother brought from the city.

"Can you believe she flew a pony in?" Elle asks as Vivian stands beside Sophie, handing her the gifts one by one.

"Yep," Dallas and Charlotte say at the same time.

"We live on a ranch, and she flew a pony in from Upstate New York. That's insane," Elle exclaims.

"That's Viv. I knew she was going to do something to try to upstage whatever Madeline and Jefferson got them for the baby," Dallas says.

"Especially seeing as they gave them a home for a wedding gift," Charlotte adds.

Jefferson Lancaster is Sophie's father. He and his second wife, Madeline, own Rustic Peak. Madeline is Braxton and Elle's aunt, and they have lived with them since their parents died in an accident when Elle was three years old. They gave a piece of land on the back side of the ranch that overlooks the river to Braxton and Sophie as a gift when they got engaged. Braxton spent the months before their wedding building their house on that land.

"It's still nuts. I thought Uncle Jefferson's head was going to explode when the trailer pulled up with that animal on it," Elle continues.

"I wish I could have been here to see that," Dallas says on a giggle. Then, she groans.

"Are you okay?" I ask.

"Yes, I think I might have just tinkled on myself a little though. Laughing always does that these days," she says.

"Ew," Charlotte says and then thinks better as she reaches over and pats Dallas's shoulder. "I mean, ah, that's sweet."

"Yep, I'm adorable," Dallas retorts as she pops another meatball in her mouth.

Once Sophie opens all her gifts and everyone has eaten their fill, we get up and start mingling under the twinkling lights.

Elle's aunt Doreen and aunt Ria are fussing over the baskets at the party-favor table.

"Hi, girls," Aunt Doreen says before rounding the table and engulfing first Dallas and then me into a big hug.

"It's so good to see you. How long are you going to be home?" she asks me.

"Through the summer. For now. I'm hoping to start a new job in a couple of months."

"That's wonderful. I know the girls are happy to have you home for a while." She beams.

"You girls make sure to take a basket. It's the only thing Vivian would let Ria and me handle."

I check out the small handwoven baskets that have a handwritten card attached that says, *Tickled Pink You Came*. Inside is a small terra-cotta flowerpot and seed packet that says, *Let Love Grow*; a bag of white chocolate–drizzled popcorn that says, *She's Ready to Pop*; along with an assortment of baked goodies, a set of white-and-pink handmade goat's milk soap bars, and a tiny bottle of pink champagne that says, *Pop It When She Pops*.

"These are amazing," I say as I snatch up two.

"Take one for your momma too. I hate that she was feeling poorly and couldn't make it. She and Miss Elaine helped us assemble the baskets after church last week. She made the popcorn, and Elaine made the soaps."

They helped Momma make the favor baskets for Dallas's shower too.

A basket full of their love.

"These are charming. You guys outdid yourselves. And this shindig, woohoo," I muse.

"It is lovely. I know Viv can be a bit much, but the woman knows how to throw a party," Aunt Doreen praises.

We hear a whistle just as Braxton, Walker, and Jefferson round the house.

Braxton beelines for Sophie, and Walker and Jefferson head our way.

Walker picks Elle up off her feet, and she squirms in his grasp.

"Yuck, you're all sweaty," she complains.

He releases her. "That's because we worked our asses off today. Now, I'm hungry. Where are those fancy sandwiches and cakes?" he asks as he looks around, and his eyes land on Dallas. "Did you eat them all?"

She scowls at him. "No, I did not, asshat," she spits at him.

He throws his hands in the air. "All right, it's nothing to get so blowed up about," he says, and Jefferson can't help but burst into laughter.

Dallas throws a punch into Walker's ribs.

"Ow, you're so sensitive," he complains as he rubs his side.

"Never mess with a pregnant woman past her due date," Dallas warns.

"How overdue are you, dear?" Aunt Ria asks.

"Four days. The doctor says if I don't go into labor by the weekend, he is going to induce me on Monday morning," Dallas informs us.

"I can't believe it's time already," I squeal.

I'm so looking forward to being an aunt. Our whole family has been bubbling with excitement awaiting our newest member's arrival.

Dallas cradles her stomach. "I know. I can't wait to meet him or her either even if I do feel like a whale that has to pee every five minutes. Speaking of, I'll be right back," she says as she waddles off in the direction of the house.

She almost makes it to the back door when she stops and turns around.

"Bellamy!" she yells as she looks down.

She is standing in a puddle.

"Whoa. Couldn't hold it, huh?" Walker shouts back.

"Oh, that's not what that is," Doreen says before turning and calling for Braxton and pointing to Dallas.

Braxton looks that direction and starts running toward her, as do I.

Walker looks confused for a second, and then he falls in beside me.

"Call Myer," I tell him, and he snatches his phone from his pocket.

I skid to a stop in front of her, and she is looking down at the mess.

"My water broke," she says shakily.

Braxton gets to us, takes one look at Dallas, and says, "I'll get my truck."

He heads to the driveway.

"I've got Myer," Walker says as he waves his phone in the air.

"Tell him Dallas is in labor and to meet us at the hospital. And tell him to stop and grab her bags," I instruct.

"He doesn't have to stop. We'll do that," Charlotte says as she and Sophie make it to us.

"Beau?" Dallas says as she looks to Sophie.

"We've got him too. We'll stop and get your stuff and be right behind you guys," Sophie assures her.

"I'm sorry I ruined your shower," Dallas whispers.

"Ruin? Are you kidding me? It's the perfect ending! You saved the best gift for last," Sophie squeals as Braxton arrives, pulling his truck to a stop right in front of us.

"Come on. Let's go have a baby," I say as I open the truck door, and Walker gently helps Dallas up into the passenger seat.

I close her in.

"I'll be right behind you in my car," I tell her before they peel out.

Cheers and whistles go up as I walk around the side of the house and watch the truck pull out of the gate.

I turn to look at everyone. They all have tears in their eyes.

"Let's go have a niece or nephew!"

Three

DALLAS'S PARENTS AND HER BROTHER, PAYNE, ARE AT THE hospital when we arrive.

Her mother follows her into the delivery room while her daddy, Payne, Braxton, and I set up in the waiting room across the hall.

Ten minutes later, I peek my head out the door and see my brother frantically making his way down the hall, headed for the nurses' station.

I step out to greet him.

"Where is she?" A breathless Myer skids to a stop in front of me with Momma and Pop in tow.

"In room 314. Relax. You have time."

"Thanks for getting her here safely," he says before he takes off toward the rooms.

"Dottie is already in there, and she wants you in there too," Mr. Henderson, who has walked up behind me, tells Momma.

Tears immediately fill her eyes, and she nods, hands her bag off to our dad and follows Myer.

I loop my arm through his as he watches Myer and Momma disappear into Dallas's room.

"Come on, Gramps. Let's go wait," I tell him, and his wet eyes are smiling as he lets me lead him into the waiting room.

One by one, our friends trickle in, and before you know it, the waiting room is running over with Dallas and Myer's thrilled family and friends—Walker and Elle, Madeline, Doreen, Ria, and Sonia. Finally, Sophie and Charlotte come in with Beau, carrying boxes.

"We brought the baby some cupcakes," Beau says as he bounces into the room and to his uncle Payne.

"Yeah, we had lots left over from the shower, so we thought we'd bring them for everyone to snack on while they waited," Sophie says as she hands off the boxes to Braxton.

"We'll run down to the cafeteria and grab coffees and sodas. Come on, Walk," Braxton offers after setting the treats on the table under the television.

"I'll be right back. I'm going to check on them," I tell the room at large before pacing down to the nurses' station.

"Any word on Dallas Wilson?" I ask the nurse who has answered this question for me several times.

She gives me a patient smile. "Not yet, dear. Last time we checked in, she was dilated to an eight."

"Okay, thank you. This is our first baby in the family. We're a little excited," I explain.

"I promise, as soon as the doctor is called in and she starts pushing, I'll come to give you guys an update," she offers.

"I appreciate that."

I head back down to the waiting room, and I hear Charlotte's voice fussing at someone.

"Seriously? That's what you wear to the hospital? You know that's what you're going to be wearing in every picture the day your niece or nephew was born, right?"

I see Payne grinning up at her with Beau sitting in his lap.

"What does it say?" Beau asks curiously.

"Nothing," Charlotte gets out just as Payne says proudly, *"Beavers love wood."*

"Payne!" Charlotte scolds.

Beau looks up at her, confused. "Beavers do love wood. They build dams in the river," he helpfully replies.

"They sure do, buddy," Payne agrees as he grins up at Charlotte.

"You're a pig," Charlotte says.

"No, he's not. He's a boy," Beau defends, and Payne's grin gets wider.

Charlotte rolls her eyes and sits down in the chair beside them.

I join Elle and Sonia in the chairs on the opposite wall.

Braxton and Walker return with trays of beverages and start passing them out to everyone.

"Hey, guys. Thanks for coming," I tell my best friends.

"Like we'd miss it. This baby is going to be calling us Auntie too," Sonia says.

"Where's Ricky?" I ask.

She sighs. "At home. He told me babies are chick territory. I texted him when we got here and told him that Walker, Braxton, and Payne were all here, but he didn't respond. Maybe I should try him again," she says as she fishes her phone from her bag. "I'm going to step outside and give him a call, see if I can convince him to ride over."

She walks off, and Walker takes her vacated seat beside Elle.

"She really wants Ricky to become friends with you guys," Elle tells Walker, and he snorts.

"Not going to happen," he says.

"Maybe he's not that bad once you get to know him better," I offer.

"Oh, they've tried. I convinced Walker to take him out for a few beers about a month after their wedding while Sonia and I had a girls' night," Elle says.

"I'm never doing that again, and no amount of sexual persuasion is going to change my mind this time," Walker insists as he cuts his eyes to Elle.

She gives him a *challenge accepted* grin.

"I mean it, woman!"

"That bad, huh?" I ask.

"The guy's an asshole. All he did was complain about everything. The bar was too loud. The beers were lukewarm. The wings were too expensive," he starts, ticking off Ricky's offenses.

"Sounds like a fun date," Braxton says as he sits across from us.

"You're much more my type," Walker says as he winks at him and blows him a kiss.

"Aw," Brax responds with a hand to his heart.

"Gross. Your bromance is falling out; you'd better tuck that back in," I rag them.

Walker chucks a cupcake topper at me before he continues, "Honestly, I have no idea what Sonia was thinking, marrying that guy. He spent the rest of the night getting hammered on those lukewarm beers and pawing at every female in the place. I swear, if I hadn't promised Elle to be on my best behavior, I would have knocked his ass out for touching them without their permission and left him bleeding on the bar floor."

"Maybe you should have," Braxton mumbles under his breath.

"That would have gone over well, coming home to me and Sonia from your boys' night out—without her husband," Elle interjects.

"She'd be better off if I had," Walker says tightly.

"Even if that were true, we have to support her and try our best to get along with him," I tell them.

"I'll be nice when he's around. I'm just not ever going to be great friends with him," Walker says.

Sonia returns, looking dejected. "He's so tired from working. He's going to chill, and he said he'll come with me to meet the baby next weekend or something. But he told me to give everyone his regards and congratulations," she says, her voice dripping with disappointment.

"That's perfect," I tell her as I pat the chair beside me. "This part is just a whole bunch of boring waiting anyway."

"You're right," she agrees.

We all sit there, gabbing and watching television. We get no news for the next three excruciating hours.

Beau wakes up from the nap he took on his Pop-Pop's chest and asks if the baby came.

"Not yet, little man. Hopefully, it won't be much longer," his grandfather, Marvin, informs him.

He sighs heavily.

"It's going to be a girl for sure," Beau mutters.

"Why do you think that?" Payne asks.

"Because it's taking so long. Girls take a long time to get ready to come out," he says like it makes perfect sense.

"He's right," Walker agrees. "It has to be a girl."

A little over an hour later, Myer emerges.

"It's a girl," he confirms as we all get to our feet.

Congratulations ring out from everyone.

"Come on, little man. Let's go meet your baby sister," Myer says as he opens his arms.

Beau flies to him, and he scoops him up off the floor. Then, he looks over to me.

"You and Payne, Marvin and Pop, too, sis. Everyone else can come in a couple of minutes," he says to me.

I rise from the chair, move to my big brother, and wrap him in my arms.

Payne, Dallas's daddy, and Pop join us, and the six of us head to the room to meet our newest family member.

When we enter, Dallas is on the bed, holding the tiny bundle in her arms. A content look on her face.

Myer sets Beau down beside them, and he crawls up to look at the baby snuggled up on his momma's chest.

"She's little," Beau says as he gets his first glimpse of his new sister.

"She sure is," Dallas agrees.

Beau takes his hand and touches the tiny smattering of hair on her head.

"She's soft," he whispers.

"She is, and that's why we have to be very gentle with her," Dallas says.

"Can I hold her?" he asks.

"Scoot up here, against the pillows, and I'll put her in your lap."

Myer protectively proceeds to the side of the bed as Dallas moves to lay the baby across Beau's lap. She keeps her hand under the baby's neck, and Myer squats down to a knee and moves in close on the other side.

Beau looks down at the squirming baby, mesmerized by her. "I'm gonna be the bestest big brother there ever was. I'll share all my toys, and I'll teach you how to ride my bicycle, and I'll save my saddle for you for when you get big like me. I won't let anybody be mean to you either," he tells her.

She coos up at him and opens her eyes for a moment.

Beau's face brightens.

"She heard me," he says.

"I'm sure she did, buddy," Myer responds.

Dallas sniffles and wipes at her eyes.

"She likes me, Mommy," he tells Dallas as he looks up at her.

"I can see that," Dallas replies.

"What's her name?" he asks.

Dallas smiles at Myer.

"I think we decided on Dorothy Faith after my momma, but we're going to call her Faith," she tells us.

"Faith," Beau repeats reverently.

He kisses the top of her head.

"You three, stay right there," I say as I take my phone from my purse.

I start snapping a million pictures of the new family.

Then, Dallas takes the wiggly baby from her brother's arms and

Beau hops down, so the rest of us can get our turns, holding little Faith.

"Really, Payne?" Dallas says as she reads his shirt.

He just grins at her, and she shakes her head. Then, he leans down and kisses her forehead.

"You did good, sis. She's beautiful."

Then, he extends his hand to Myer. "How's your hand, man? You okay to shake?" he asks.

"Yeah. Why?" Myer asks as he takes his brother-in-law's offered hand.

"Because I played coach last go-around, and she almost crushed mine to dust."

"That's because I wasn't able to get the epidural last time, and you were getting on my last nerve," Dallas snaps.

I take the baby and walk over to the window that overlooks a field full of colorful wildflowers.

"Hey, Faith. I'm your auntie Bells, and we are going to be great friends. No matter what, I will always have your back, even against your own mommy and daddy, if you need me to. I'll have the fun house you come to stay at, and you will always be my favorite girl in the whole wide world," I whisper to my new niece. "Thank you for waiting for me to get home before you came out to play."

I kiss the top of her head, and she lets out a small whimper.

And just like that, I'm in love.

Myer comes to my side and smiles down at us.

"So, a baby girl. Sorry, big brother, I know you were hoping for a boy to teach how to ride and throw a football."

He shakes his head. "I already have my boy. She's exactly what I prayed for—a little girl who's a spitfire like her momma and as strong as all the other women in my life. I'm a blessed man to be surrounded by beautiful females," he says as he kisses the side of my head.

We get a few more minutes together before the room is flooded with everyone. Walker and Braxton walk in with their arms full of flowers and stuffed animals, and Sophie heads straight for me with her arms out. I relinquish the baby to her.

"Meet Faith, Auntie Sophie," I say as I hand her over.

"Faith. Oh, I love it. You and our Lily Claire are going to be besties," she tells the baby, and then she bursts into tears.

Braxton comes and wraps his arm around her shoulders.

"What's wrong, Miss Sophie?" Beau asks.

"She's just happy, buddy," Braxton tells him.

Then, one by one, every woman in the room starts losing their own battle with happy tears.

Beau looks around in alarm.

"Women," Walker says as he scoops Beau up. "They're all crazy."

Beau just nods his head in agreement and giggles.

"All right, everyone, let's clear out and let Myer and Dallas and Faith get some rest." Beverly urges us all to the door.

"Yes, we can all use a little beauty sleep," Sophie agrees before handing the baby back off to Dallas.

"Beauty sleep? Woman, look at how pretty I am. I get any prettier, and no one will be able to stand to look at me!" Walker says as Elle nudges him forward.

"I already can't stand to look at you, dipshit!" Charlotte says as she falls in behind them.

"Night, Dal," he says as he is shoved out the door.

"Night, guys."

Four

MOMMA AND I SPENT SUNDAY COOKING A BUNCH OF MEALS to freeze and put in Myer and Dallas's freezer.

Today, I'm up with the chickens to start work.

Pop insisted that Myer take the next two weeks off from the ranch to help Dallas at home. So, I'm going to be pitching in as much as possible. I can't do a lot of the harder work, but I can clean stalls with the best of them. Plus, Momma and I are going to be helping Mrs. Henderson look after Beau when she is at the bakery.

"I'm here. Where do you guys want me?" I ask as I enter the barn.

Pop is loading a truck with hay bales as Foster and Truett toss them down from the loft. Foster and Truett have worked at Stoney Ridge for Pop for as long as I can remember. They are my brother's age and started when they were in high school.

"If you could feed and water the horses, that'd be a big help," he says as he lifts another bale and drops it next to the others.

"Sure thing." I grab one of the buckets by the sink and start to fill it with fresh water.

He stops and looks my way. "It's sure nice to have you home for a while, sweetheart."

"It's good to be home, Pop. Just don't get used to it."

"I won't; I won't. But I will enjoy having my whole family together while I can," he says before shutting the tailgate.

I smile at him. It's nice to be home too.

Foster and Truett descend the ladder and join him.

"We're off to fill the feedlots, but hopefully, we'll be back before Dr. Haralson gets here to check on the mare in the foaling stall. If not, we shouldn't be far behind," Pop tells me before they all hop into the truck and drive out of the back of the barn.

Oh boy, another baby is coming.

I spend the next couple of hours getting my work done, and once all the horses are fed and watered, I check and pick their hooves before turning them out into the pasture for a little sunshine and exercise.

As I head to the house for lunch, I see a Range Rover coming down the drive. I stop and wait for it to arrive. It halts, and Brandt Haralson—our new vet in Poplar Falls—emerges. He walks over to help his mother, Miss Elaine, out of the passenger side.

"Hi, Bellamy." Miss Elaine waves as she makes her way to me.

"Hi yourself," I greet.

"I decided to ride out with Brandt and visit with your mother while he tends to the birth," she explains.

"She'll love that. In fact, you have perfect timing. She and I are about to have lunch out on the porch. Pop and the boys should be back at any time. You two, come join us until they get here," I invite.

"We don't mean to impose on your lunch," she starts.

"Oh, please. Momma cooks enough for an army. She'll be tickled pink you guys are here," I say, brushing off her apology.

We reach the steps just as Momma comes out of the door with a tablecloth in hand.

"Elaine, how wonderful. You're just in time for my Brunswick stew and corn bread." She beams.

"See, I told you," I whisper as I nudge her side.

She joins Momma and I wait for Brandt to make it to us.

"Hiya, handsome. Come to make me an auntie again this week, I see," I say as he approaches.

He smiles, and his green eyes twinkle in the sunlight.

"Yes, ma'am. How are Dallas and the baby doing, by the way?" he inquires.

"Wonderful. Little Faith is perfect, and Dallas is a natural at this mommy gig," I praise.

"I had no doubt she would be after knowing Beau," he agrees.

"Yeah, he's pretty special. Are you hungry?" I ask.

"Not at all, but thank you for inviting Mom. If you point me in the direction of the mare, I'll go ahead and check on her progress."

"Just follow me, and I'll show you," I say as I gesture toward the barn.

I call up to tell Momma I'll be back for lunch, and I usher Brandt to the foaling stall.

"So, how are you liking Poplar Falls?" I make small talk as we walk.

Brandt moved here from Oregon to take over the practice from the town's previous vet last year. Dr. Sherrill had been tending to all the critters in Poplar Falls since before I was born and finally decided to retire at seventy.

"It's a good town, full of good people. Mom has made some great friends and seems happy here," he says in answer.

I don't miss how he fails to mention if he is happy.

"And you?" I push.

A patient smile forms, and he looks straight ahead as he speaks, "I'm content."

Hmm, content. Not exactly happy, but not unhappy.

I know that he and Elle went out on several dates before she and Walker started their relationship. Perhaps he had hoped that would pan out in the future, but their engagement news squashed that.

"Well, you never know, Doc. That contentment might turn in to flat-out happiness before you realize it's happening," I encourage.

He cuts his eyes to me. "Maybe," he says.

I can't read him. He's closed off tighter than a duck's ass. Which intrigues me, so I keep digging.

"What's your story, Doc?"

"My story?" he asks, confused.

"Your story. I know you have one. It's written all over you. Maybe if you get it off your chest, you'll feel better. I'm no counselor or anything, but I was raised by a bunch of nosy women who always found a way to make me talk. It worked at helping my friends and me with all our teen drama, so I figure there must be something to it," I explain.

"Teen drama," he repeats.

"Frivolous, I know, but doesn't discount the benefit of getting things off your chest," I defend.

He nods thoughtfully. "I'll keep that in mind."

He humors me as we approach the barn, and it becomes clear from the sound the mare is making that it's in distress.

"She was fine a few minutes ago," I tell him as we take off at a hurried pace, our conversation lost in the urgency.

We make it to the barn, and he follows me to the large stall in the back.

"Stay here," he commands as he opens the door and enters cautiously.

"Is she okay?" I ask as I peek over the door.

The mare is on her side, and she is rolling on the floor of the stall in agony.

"She's in full-on labor, and she's trying to get the foal in position," he tells me as he opens his messenger bag and pulls out elbow-length medical gloves.

He quickly rolls his shirtsleeves and gloves up.

The expectant mother gets to her feet and is obviously in a lot of pain.

Over the years, I've witnessed a lot of births from horses and cows. Even I know that something is not right at the moment.

Brandt holds the lead rope and tries to stead the animal so that he can examine her. She won't settle, so I open the stall and carefully walk in at an angle to let her know I am approaching. I speak softly to her and gently take the rope from his hand.

"Easy, there. Everything is going to be okay."

He gives me an appreciative glance before moving to her hindquarters.

"Shit," he mutters, and I know that my assumption was correct.

"What's wrong?" I ask.

"The foal is breech," he answers as the mare bears up.

"Shh, it's okay, girl. We are here to help you and your baby." I try to soothe the momma-to-be.

"What now?" I ask, doing my best to keep my voice even.

"I have to attempt to get its hind legs back into the uterus, so I can turn it. If not, we could lose them both," he says.

"Oh no. Please, please, please, Lord," I whisper the plea.

"Try to keep her calm," he instructs, and I watch as he goes elbow deep.

He wrestles with the baby for what seems like hours, but it has to be more like ten to fifteen minutes. I do the best I can to keep the mare steady and calm, but she is clearly in agony.

"Doc, I don't know if I can hold on to her much longer," I confess as my arms grow weak and I start to lose my grip.

"Hang on a few more minutes, Momma," he says to the horse.

Then, he looks over to me and says calmly, "The foal is in now, and I need to get it turned before the compression on the umbilical cord cuts off its oxygen. Move around here slowly. I might need help with pulling the baby out," he commands, and I do as he said quickly.

I can see the ripple of power move through his shoulders and across his back, and he uses his entire body to twist the baby as gently as he can.

"Is it moving?" I ask.

"Yes, but I have to be careful, so I don't tear her wall," he answers.

I stand behind him and wait as he uses all his strength to get the baby in the right position.

Minutes later, I can see the front legs emerge, and I let out the breath I was holding. I have seen enough births to know this is what we want.

He pulls back and makes room for me to his right. I grab the baby's legs as he rolls his hands underneath, and together, we tug until we see the eyes and snout of the foal. I can feel when the mare's normal contractions begin, and her body strains to help us expel her baby. Once it's out, Brandt quickly removes his gloves and reaches for a large piece of straw. I watch anxiously as he swabs the baby's nose to clear its airway.

"Come on now. Breathe for me, little one," he prompts.

A few seconds later, the foal releases a tiny sneeze, and its chest begins to rise and fall.

"Is it okay?" I ask as I sit back in the straw, watching him work.

"He's small. But I think he'll make it," he says as he turns to look at me with a triumphant smile on his face.

He. It's a colt.

"Come here, Bellamy." He beckons as he reaches out to me, and I take his hand. "I need you to count its breaths."

He places my hand on its rib cage, and I start to track the in-and-out movements while he pulls a watch from his bag. I count, and he times.

"Is that a good rate?" I ask about the respiration.

"Perfect," he says, and he smiles a relieved smile at me.

"Oh, thank God," I say as I watch the little guy struggle to open his eyes.

Pop and Foster come rushing into the barn a moment later.

Pop takes us in. We are both on the floor of the stall, exhausted and covered in slime, with the babe between us. What a sight we must be.

"Foster, get that mare washed down quickly, and I'll grab the colostrum bottle," Pop barks.

I stand, and Foster enters with wash buckets and sponges.

Pop hands off a feeding bottle to Brandt, and he promptly coaxes the colt to suckle. Once he latches on, Pop places his hand on my shoulder.

"Are you okay, sweetheart?" he asks.

"Yeah, I'm great now that the little one is here and is going to be okay."

"We've got it from here. Go get cleaned up and have some lunch," he tells me.

I nod and turn toward the door.

"You did good, Bellamy," Brandt calls after me.

"Me? I didn't do anything. You just saved them," I say in awe.

"I couldn't have done it without your help," he states before he looks back down and starts tending to the patient.

"I think you should get to name him, Bells," Pop says.

I look at the newborn lying in front of Brandt, and I say, "Ali. His name is Ali. He's a little fighter."

"Ali it is," Pop proclaims.

I walk to the house, filled with joy at watching that baby struggle to make it into this world and a little in awe of our handsome vet. That is the first breech birth I've witnessed on this ranch, where both momma and baby survived.

Five

BELLAMY

I MAKE MY WAY BACK TO THE HOUSE AND FIND MOMMA AND MISS Elaine chatting over coffee.

"Bellamy, what in the world happened?" Momma asks as I climb the steps.

"I had to help Brandt deliver a breech foal," I offer in explanation of my appearance.

"My goodness, is everything all right?"

"Yep, Doc was amazing, and he was able to save them both," I praise.

"Thank the good Lord. Oh, honey, you go get yourself cleaned up, and I'll heat you up some lunch."

I scurry into the house, and enjoy a long, hot shower before I rejoin them on the porch in clean clothes, my hair still damp.

Momma sets a bowl of hot stew in front of me, and I devour it in minutes. She offers me seconds.

"I guess delivering babies makes you hungry," she muses.

"Ravenous. I hope you have enough for Brandt. He deserves a whole pot to himself. He was amazing out there," I tell them, still filled with admiration for the doctor.

"Is that so?" Momma asks as she brings her eyes to Miss Elaine.

"Yes, ma'am. You should have seen him. He kept his cool, and before I knew what was happening, he'd saved that mare's and colt's lives. I was scared out of my mind, but he was steady as a rock. It was like watching a superhero in action or something," I recount for them. Reverence clear in my tone.

"That's his job," Miss Elaine states. "It amazes me every time I see a sick animal with a distraught owner come through the doors of our clinic and then leave with a new lease on life. That boy makes me proud every day."

"How is the clinical practice?" Momma asks.

"Busy. Too busy for me sometimes. He had a mixed practice in Oregon, too, but he wasn't the only vet in town, so it wasn't that stressful. If he was out on large-animal calls, our vet techs would see to the routine visits, and if there was an after-hours emergency, there was an emergency clinic about twenty minutes away," she explains.

"Maybe he should look into hiring a technician to help out," Momma suggests.

"It's part of the plan. We've just been so busy that we haven't had a chance to start looking properly. I intended to go home and visit my daughter and grandchildren for a couple of weeks this month while they were out of school, but I can't leave him without any help."

"I can help," I offer.

Both their eyes come to me.

"I mean, I can work temporarily while you go for your visit. I promised Pop I'd help out here on the ranch until Myer returned from paternity leave, but after that, I'm free for a few weeks. I won't be leaving for Denver until the end of summer. That is, if you trust me to do a good job."

"That's a wonderful idea," Momma says. "She has a degree in animal science, and she's great with animals, has been since she was a little girl. She's a perfect candidate to help in a veterinary clinic."

"Are you sure you want to spend what's left of your summer break working?" Miss Elaine asks, but I can hear the hope in her question.

I shrug. "Sure. It's only a couple of weeks, right? Besides, maybe I can even talk Dr. Haralson into calling in a personal recommendation on my behalf afterward."

"I'm sure he would be happy to," Miss Elaine assures me.

"Then, we'll talk to Brandt, and if he agrees, you can call your daughter and make arrangements," I tell her as she beams at me.

"Thank you, dear."

Once the men finish up in the barn, Pop and Foster walk Brandt up to the house to fetch his mother.

Momma forces stew on him, after he cleans up a bit, and he humors her and has a big bowl and a slice of corn bread.

We discuss me filling in for Miss Elaine while she takes a trip home, and he readily agrees.

"Thanks. I can use the experience," I tell him as I walk with them to his SUV before they head back to town.

He looks back at his mother while she hugs my momma.

"Actually, thank you, Bellamy. She could use this break. She loves it here in Colorado, but I know she misses the kids and her friends back home. It'll be good for her to get away and see them."

"Do you? Miss home, I mean," I ask.

"Oregon? Nope, not in the least," he says matter-of-factly.

"Good, because I think Poplar Falls wants to keep you," I tell him.

That gets me a happy crinkle at his eyes.

"Brandt," Pop calls as he approaches with his hand extended. "I appreciate all you did today."

Brandt takes the offered hand and shakes it firmly. "My pleasure. Just keep an eye on her for the next hour or so, and if she has any problems passing her placenta, give me a ring, and I'll come check her out."

"Will do."

Miss Elaine joins us, and Brandt opens the door for her. She climbs in and looks back at me.

"Drop by the clinic anytime you have a few minutes to spare, and I'll run over the basics with you," she tells me.

"Perfect. I'll swing in sometime this week."

Brandt rounds the Rover, and they back out. We stand and wave until they make the turn out of the gate.

"I think we got a good one with him," Pop observes.

"Yeah, me too," I agree.

"Well, cowgirl, are you ready to finish this day?" he asks as he wraps his arm around my shoulders and pulls me into his side.

"I am," I say, and I let him lead me back to the barn, where the evening chores await us.

Six

BRANDT

"**T**HANK YOU, SIR."

I shake Mr. Stroupe's hand before he stands and passes me a manila envelope with all the paperwork tucked inside.

"Congratulations, Brandt. You got yourself a fine piece of property. I think you are going to love raising a family there," the bank manager offers as he walks me to the door of his office.

I just purchased an old estate fifteen minutes from downtown. I had driven by the place a dozen times while making calls, and there was just something about it that spoke to me. The property is overgrown, and the house is in a state of severe disrepair, but I can tell that it was once magnificent. I know in my gut that it can be again even if I don't know the home's story. I just felt compelled to buy it and help restore it to its former glory.

I'm not sure what I was thinking, and I have a brief moment of regret as I toss the envelope into the passenger seat of my vehicle. It's probably going to take a lot of time and money to fix that place up. Of course, I have nothing better to do. The small apartment above the clinic is not what I promised Mom when I convinced her to move with me. I want her to have a real home to retire in. Somewhere she has a yard to fill with flowers and for her dog, Lou-Lou, to run around in. One with a big kitchen and maybe a she-shed in the back for her to make her soaps and lotions.

As I turn down Main Street, Mr. Phillips waves as he exits the hardware store, and Mrs. Pickens looks up and smiles at me as she sweeps the gazebo outside the courthouse. Then, I see Mr. Henderson leaving Bountiful Harvest Bread Company with Beau Wilson, tightly gripping one of his hands, while Beau licks the ice cream that's dripping from a cone off the other. And I know that Poplar Falls is where I want to lay roots.

I feel that numbing pain in my chest at that thought. *Roots*. I planted them once before, and they were yanked from the soil that was my life. They've been exposed and withering ever since. It's been hard to pull myself back together, and I'm not there yet, but making this purchase is a huge step forward. Maybe I'll be able to restore both of us.

I swing into the parking space behind the clinic and enter through the back door.

Mom is sitting at the desk on the phone, with Lou-Lou lying at her feet, and she turns as I approach.

She raises her eyebrows in question, and I wave the envelope in my hand.

Her eyes fall to the paperwork, and she smiles hugely. She turns back and finishes the call as I walk to my office and grab my lab coat. I have three appointments here this afternoon before I have to head out to give some vaccines at a farm outside of town.

I hear her hurried footfalls as she reaches my door.

"Everything went through? You bought it?"

"Yes, ma'am. Since the property was owned by the bank, they accepted my cash offer on the spot."

I made a lowball offer, sight unseen. No inspection. No haggle. I figured I'd salvage what I could of the bones of the main house and tear down everything else and build from there. Mr. Stroupe assured me the septic had been serviced and inspected recently and that a new well had been dug last year. That was enough for me. I followed my gut, and now, for better or worse, I am the proud new owner of a huge chunk of land in the Rocky Mountains.

"Wonderful!" she exclaims as we hear the bell above the front door chime.

She turns on her heels and hurries back to greet our client.

"Is it bad, Doctor?" Ms. Krause asks as I examine her white Maine Coon.

"He might have scratched his cornea, and it's caused irritation. That's why the eye is red and oozing. Or it could be a bacterial infection. I'm going to get a swab of the discharge and take a better look, and we'll get a blood sample to send off to the lab, just to rule out anything more serious. But I'm ninety-nine percent sure it's nothing an antibiotic and eyedrops can't fix," I assure the nervous cat owner.

She sighs in relief. "Thank goodness. Hazel is my best friend, aren't you, boy?" she coos at the large cat.

"Hazel?" I ask.

"Yes, I named him before I knew he was a boy. He was a little ball of white kitten fur, and he just looked like a Hazel. My husband complained about his name until the day he passed," she explains.

"I think it suits him just fine. If you want to check out with Mom up front, I'll finish up here, and I'll bring Hazel out to you."

She scratches the cat behind his ear before exiting the exam room.

I put a few numbing drops in Hazel's right eye, do a quick eye swab, and collect a blood sample, and then I pick him up and carry him out to Ms. Krause in the waiting area.

"Here you go." I hand the pet off to her.

"We'll give you a call in a couple of days with the results. Until then, here are some eyedrops to help with the discomfort. You can put them in the affected eye twice a day. We'll call out for any other prescriptions needed once we know exactly what we are dealing with, and you can swing by and pick those up next week."

"He already looks better," she cries as she cuddles Hazel close to her.

"He's going to be just fine," I tell her.

"Thank you, Dr. Haralson. You're a doll." She places Hazel in the carrier to take him home. "Bye, Miss Elaine. We'll see you next visit," she calls down the hallway to Mom.

The bell above the door chimes again, and Bellamy Wilson breezes into the office.

"Bellamy!" Ms. Krause calls.

She comes fully in and stops in front of the elderly woman.

"Well, hello. How are you and Mr. Hazel today?" Bellamy asks as she reaches into the carrier and pets the cat.

He closes his eyes and purrs loudly.

"Oh, we're okay. He just has a little eye infection, but Dr. Haralson is getting him all patched up."

"That's good to hear," she says as she smiles a beautiful smile at the pair.

In fact, everything about her is beautiful, not just her smile.

She has her long hair pulled back in a ponytail, which hangs through the back of a charcoal-gray ball cap that says, *Charm and Chaos*. She's wearing a pair of well-worn, faded jeans, which have ripped knees, topped with a tight sage-green Stoney Ridge Ranch T-shirt and finished off with gray hiking sandals. Her blue eyes are dancing underneath a fan of long, dark lashes. She's makeup-free, and yet her face is absolutely glowing.

I catch Ms. Krause's eye as she watches me watching Bellamy.

"Well?" she asks me.

"Well?" I say.

"Dear, Bellamy asked if you were busy at the moment," she says and nods encouragement for me to answer.

I clear my throat and speak, flustered that I was caught staring, "No, not busy. We're done here for the day. I'm heading out to make a house call." I avoid Ms. Krause's curious expression and direct my response to Bellamy. "How can we help you today, Miss Wilson?"

"I was just on my way out to Rustic Peak and thought I'd drop in, so your mom could give me a quick office tutorial, if she has the time," she says as she blinks up at me.

"Are you working here now, Bellamy?" Ms. Krause interrupts.

"I'm just going to fill in for a couple of weeks while Doc's mom is on vacation."

"How lovely. Oh, there is my ride. Give Winston and Beverly my regards, won't you, dear?" she says as Bellamy holds the door open for her.

"Yes, ma'am."

She waits until Ms. Krause is safely in the minivan that pulled up to the curb, waves good-bye, and then shuts the door, turning back to me.

"So, where do we start?"

"Mom's in the break room. Follow me," I say and then lead her to the small break room in the back of the clinic.

When we walk in, Mom is sitting at the table in the center of the room, watching one of her daytime soaps while stirring cream into her coffee.

"Bellamy," she greets.

"Hi, Miss Elaine. Is this a good time to go over your procedures?"

"Oh, yes. We just finished with our last in-clinic patient of the day, so I'm free—after I find out who the John Doe who just checked into General Hospital actually is. Come sit. Would you like a cup of coffee?" Mom asks.

"No, thank you, but please enjoy yours. I can wait. Besides, I'm willing to bet money that patient is a long-lost Cassadine," Bellamy says as she takes a seat.

Mom's eyes go round. "You think so?" she asks, excited at the prospect.

"Um, I'll leave you two to it, then. It was good to see you again, Bellamy," I say before excusing myself.

"You too, Brandt," she says on a smile.

I make it all the way back to my office before I realize I have a goofy grin on my face.

Seven

BELLAMY

AFTER MISS ELAINE GIVES ME A BRIEF RUNDOWN OF THE clinic's day-to-day operation, I head out to Rustic Peak to meet with Elle, Sonia, and Sophie. They are in cahoots to plan a surprise sixty-fifth birthday party for Doreen. Sophie doesn't want her aunt's big day to be lost in the chaos of her pregnancy and Elle's engagement, and she knows Doreen will insist they don't make a big fuss over her, so we have to run a covert operation. Which isn't easy. The Lancaster women are all-knowing, and to surprise one of them with anything is nearly impossible.

I walk into the ranch's office above the barn, and the summit is already in progress.

"There's no way to have it here. We'd never be able to get her gone long enough to set up without her asking too many questions. Besides, as soon as she pulled up the driveway and saw everyone's vehicles, she'd figure it out. I want us to actually be able to hide and jump out and yell, *Surprise*," Sophie says as I take a seat on the sofa next to Sonia.

"You could have it at the church recreation hall. Lie to her and say it's a ladies' meeting or something. Then, she would be expecting a parking lot full of cars," Sonia offers what sounds like a solid plan.

"We can't dance or drink at the church, and I want to be able to do both," Elle mumbles.

"I agree," Sophie says. "I kind of want to do a fifties theme. You know, like *Grease*-esque. Poodle skirts and saddle shoes. That sort of thing."

"Oh, I love that idea," I agree.

"I bet Momma could make the poodle skirts," Sonia adds.

"And Dallas's dad has that old jukebox out on his back porch. I bet it still works if we can gather together a bunch of forty-five vinyl records," I inform them.

"Doreen and Ria have a ton of them up in the attic. They used to listen to them all the time, but the old record player's needle broke, and they kept intending to have it fixed but never did," Elle says.

"The men could all basically dress as themselves. Just add some grease to their hair. Maybe they won't complain too much," Sophie adds.

"Right." I laugh, imagining my brother and his friends adding product to their heads.

"They'll get over it. It's for Doreen," Elle insists.

"So, where do we do it, and how do we get her there, unaware?" Sophie asks us all.

"Maybe we let her know there's a party. Just don't let her know it's for her," I suggest.

They cut their eyes to me.

"Okay, we're listening," Sophie prompts.

"Elle did just get engaged, and we didn't have a proper celebration because … well, Sonia got married, I had to go back to school, and then you and Dallas had baby showers. Elle's engagement kind of got lost in the shuffle." I shrug.

"Oh, goodness, Elle. We did brush your happy announcement under the rug. I'm so sorry," Sophie cries as her eyes fill with tears and she grasps Elle's hand.

Elle turns her annoyed eyes to me. "Look what you did. You made a pregnant lady cry."

"I'm sorry," I snap.

"I'm not upset, Sophie. I don't need an engagement party. We don't really do those here anyway. The only reason you had one is because Vivian had insisted. You guys can gush all over me at my bridal shower."

"My point is," I start again, "we can tell Doreen we are throwing Elle and Walker a surprise engagement party. If she's in on it, we can have it wherever we want, and we can make it her job to get Elle to the party without ruining the surprise. That way, we can all be there, getting things set up, and Doreen can spend the day finding ways to distract Elle. Then, when they arrive, we can all be like, *Surprise! We got you, Doreen!*"

They all stare at me with their mouths agape.

Then, Sophie finally whispers, "That's kind of brilliant."

"I know, right?" I declare proudly. "I can do brilliant occasionally."

"Okay, so, Sonia, you talk to your mom about making skirts. Elle, you work on the guest list and get the number and sizes to her. I'll start looking for a venue and get Dallas to ask her dad about the jukebox."

"Sonia and I will bring it up to Doreen sometime tonight since we are spending the night. We'll tell her that Walker wants to throw the party for Elle, and we'll get her input on when and the food, et cetera. So, we'll know her preferences, and have everything she wants," I suggest.

"Just make sure it's about six weeks out. That's right before her birthday, so she won't clue in. Plus, I want Dallas to be recovered and be able to be there," Sophie instructs.

"Got it. When are you due again?" I ask.

"In nine weeks, so I should be good," she assures.

"That, or we'll just have another baby at the end of a party. As we do," Sonia says.

"No. No, no, no. I want the night to be all about Aunt Doe," Sophie declares as she stands and points at her bump. "So, you just stay put, missy."

We all stand with her, and she heads to the door before turning back to us.

"I'll go let Aunt Ria in on the plan now, so she'll know to play along. I'm so excited. Aunt Doe loves parties, and she deserves to be celebrated."

After our secret meeting, Sonia, Elle, and I head to the main house to help with dinner.

"It's so nice to have every one of you girls here under one roof again. I miss all those study sessions and slumber parties when you three were in middle and high school. You all grew up too fast. Moving off and getting married and finding jobs," Aunt Doreen says as she opens the oven and checks on the chicken roasting inside.

"I miss those days too. I haven't any idea why we were in such a hurry to grow up and get out on our own. If I could go back, knowing what I know now, I'd want to start at fourteen, do it all over again, and enjoy that time more. Live in the moment instead of missing it by chasing after the future. Honestly, high school is a blur," Sonia says.

"That's why they say, *Youth is wasted on the young.* You're too immature to appreciate that you have lots of energy and beauty and debt-free, carefree lives. You think everything is a big deal. Every fight with your friends and every boy who breaks your heart. In hindsight, most of your disagreements were over silly things, and you'll fall in and out of love many times before you find your soul mate," Doreen muses.

"You believe in soul mates, Doreen?" I ask.

"I do. And I believe you can have more than one in a lifetime too."

"Isn't that contradictory?" Sonia asks.

"No, not at all. I believe God leads us to the right people, the ones who enhance our lives and build us up and make us feel whole, but if we in our eagerness make a hasty choice, or that love is lost, be it through circumstance or death, I believe he is merciful and he can bring a second chance back around," she says.

"But aren't you supposed to only have one husband?" Sonia asks.

"At a time, yes."

Elle and I start to giggle.

Doreen stops and turns to face us. All amusement is gone. "The Bible says it is not good for man to be alone. And the marriage vows say *until death do us part* because the Lord knows that life is fragile and there are many reasons a partner might be taken too soon. God doesn't want us to walk around, grieving forever. As long as he wakes us up every morning, he wants us to live and to be joyful. So, he can open another door to love," she explains.

"And sometimes, the last thing you want to do is put up with another man, so God sends you a huge garden and a Netflix subscription to keep you happy," Aunt Ria interjects, and we all burst into laughter.

"What are you hens cackling about?" Pop Lancaster, Sophie's grandfather, asks as he enters the kitchen door.

"Ria being an old spinster," Doreen answers.

"My Maria is no spinster. She's a smart woman who knows who she is and what she wants but, more importantly, what she doesn't want."

"Thank you, Daddy." Ria beams at him.

"What about you, Pop? Do you think you'll ever find yourself another sweetheart?" Elle asks.

"I ain't lookin' for one, but if a pretty lady comes along and wants to bless me with her company for supper, I won't turn my nose up at her either. I'm still a man, and pretty ladies are my weakness," he says with a wink before walking out.

"I can't imagine Pop with anyone other than Gram," Elle squeals as she covers her eyes.

Gram passed away a couple years ago. She and Pop Lancaster were high school sweethearts who married and raised a family together.

"Gram would be pleased if he found someone to keep him company. You don't think she'd want him to mope around, missing her constantly, do you?" Doreen asks.

"No, I don't," Elle admits. "But another woman? That would be hard to watch."

"There is nothing wrong with keeping on, moving forward in life. It's what we are supposed to do as long as we are able," Doreen advises.

"Hopefully, I never have to find out. Walker Reid would be a hard act to follow," Elle says before she stands. "I'll be right back. Nature calls."

Aunt Doreen waits until she is out of sight before she adds, "That's the truth. I don't think she'd be able to find someone to fill that boy's boots."

"Speaking of," I say in a low voice, "Sonia and I need your and Aunt Ria's help. Walker wants to throw Elle a surprise party to celebrate their engagement."

Both of the women grin conspiratorially, and I know we have Aunt Doreen right where we want her.

Game on.

Eight

BRANDT

I WAKE WITH A START. SOAKED IN SWEAT AND MY HEART RACING.

I look over at the clock beside my bed. Two o'clock. It's the same thing every time. The same nightmare that haunts me.

I lie back and get my breathing under control as I try desperately to fall asleep, but it's useless.

Sleep is an elusive fantasy. I've been exhausted for years now.

I click on the lamp that sits on the nightstand beside my bed, and I pick up the photo album that rests beside it.

I open it and relive the painful memories it holds once again. Memories that had held so much joy but now just remind me of what a fuckup I am.

This album was a gift from Annie, made for me by hand when I received my doctorate. It's a scrapbook full of photographs from high school graduation, a twenty-first birthday celebration, getting down on one knee in the sand, cutting a wedding cake, receiving the keys to our dream house and then to my first practice. All the picture-perfect moments that add up to a bunch of emptiness and nothing. A life that doesn't belong to me anymore.

I toss the book across the room, and it crashes against the wall before landing on the floor with a hollow thud.

I hear the sound of the floor creaking down the hall and am instantly filled with remorse as I see the light flicker on beneath my bedroom door.

"Brandt, are you all right, son?" My mother's soft, concerned voice drifts into the silence.

"I'm fine, Mom. Go back to sleep," I bite out, my voice hoarse from screaming in my dream.

"Another nightmare?"

I wish I could tell her no. I wish I could spare her from the worry that plagues her. Sometimes, I wake up before the conclusion of the scene, and I'm able to spend the rest of the night lost in my head without disturbing her, but on nights like tonight, when I have to watch as my heart is being ripped from my chest, there is no hiding. I'm raw and unguarded, and she knows, like a mother does, that I am hurting.

"Yes," I whisper because even though I wish she hadn't been awakened, I'm glad she is there.

"I'll make some warm milk," she says through the door.

I know she is making her way to the small kitchen to put on a pot, just like she used to when I couldn't sleep as a child. Just like she's done many nights in the last three years.

I make my way to the kitchen and sit at the small table while my mother fusses over me.

"Here you go, sweetheart. This should help," she says as she sets the steaming cup in front of me.

Oh, if only it were that easy.

"I'm sorry for waking you again, Mom," I whisper as I blow over my milk and take a comforting sip.

She pats my shoulder. "It's okay, son. It's been a few days since you had a nightmare. I was hoping that they were starting to subside," she says. "Maybe I should cancel my trip."

"No, ma'am," I cut her off. "I appreciate your concern, but I'm a grown man. I can handle myself. I have to learn to deal with the sleep-less nights. I'll even make my own warm milk," I assure her.

"I know you can, son. I just hate for you to have to. I'm your mother, and you will always be my baby boy. I will always want to chase the bad dreams away for you," she argues.

"They aren't as bad as they used to be," I lie to her.

She reaches and takes my hand in hers. "One day, you will heal, Brandt. It doesn't seem like it now, but it will happen. Trust me, I know."

I squeeze her hand and nod in agreement, but I don't think I ever will.

I don't deserve to heal.

Nine

"OH MY GOODNESS, SHE IS TOO PERFECT," I COO AS I count my niece's fingers and toes.

"She's a little diva who thinks every night is party time, and then she sleeps it off all day like a bar-hopping twenty-one-year-old sleeping off a hangover—that's what she is," Dallas corrects.

I giggle.

"Do you keep your mommy and daddy up all night? That's not very nice, Miss Faith," I tell the baby.

She blinks up at me, and a smile spreads across her face.

"Look, I know it's probably just gas but …" I move, so Dallas can see the sweet smile on her daughter's face.

"Nope, that's definitely a smirky smile. The little stinker knows exactly what she's doing, and she thinks it's funny. Don't ya, Sleeping Beauty?"

One tiny eye pops open, and her smile widens before she snuggles in deeper and falls back into a blissful slumber.

"See!" Dallas declares.

I stopped in to visit with the girls while Myer took Beau out for a ride on his new horse. When they return, Auntie Bells has a fun-filled afternoon planned for Beau, so the new parents can hopefully get a little rest.

I help Dallas give Faith her bath. Afterward, just as I get her diaper on, the front door swings open, and Beau and his chocolate Lab, Cowboy, come barreling in with Myer on their heels.

They run straight for me and the baby on a blanket on the living room floor.

Beau kisses Faith's head, and Cowboy sniffs her head before lying down next to her.

"Did you miss me, lil baby sister? I missed you," Beau says, leaning in about an inch from her face.

"Back up, Beau. I told you, you don't have to get that close. She can hear you," Dallas scolds.

Beau scoots back a hair and continues to talk to her.

Her eyes open wide, and she starts kicking her legs, watching her brother in rapt fascination. Then, she starts to form an O with her lips, making gurgling sounds.

Dallas walks over and watches them. "She only does that for him. She gets so excited when she hears his voice. She's too small to be able to turn her neck and look for him, but if he walks into a room and starts babbling, her eyes perk right up, and I can tell she is trying to search for him. When he talked to my tummy while she was cooking, she used to kick up a storm too. It's the strangest thing."

"It's because I'm her favorite person," Beau says matter-of-factly.

"I thought I was her favorite?" I say and stick my bottom lip out in a faux pout.

Beau shakes his head. "You can be her fifth favorite. I'm first, then Daddy, then Mommy, and then Cowboy," he whispers.

"I heard that," Dallas says, "and I'd better be both your and her favorite."

She pokes a finger into his ribs. Then, she gets down on the floor with us and starts tickling him and kissing him all over his face as he squirms and complains.

"At least you made the list ahead of the dog," I grumble.

After he catches his breath, Dallas tells Beau to go clean up and grab a bag because he will be staying the night with Momma and Pop and me.

"I am?" he asks excitedly.

"Yep, you and I are going to pick up Elle and then go check on the progress over at Mr. Walker's house. Then, we are going to try and talk him into taking us all fishing out on the boat."

"Yay! Pop-Pop bought me my own rod!" He jumps up and races toward the stairs.

"I'll go help him pack," Myer says as he follows him up to his room.

"Have you gotten any news on the job front yet?" Dallas asks as she drops one shoulder of her pajama shirt, and I pass Faith off to nurse.

"Not yet. They should be making the decision sometime this week. I'm going to call the head of the department on Friday if I haven't heard anything by then. It's hard. I'm trying not to be pushy and impatient, but I want to know so badly. I put all my eggs in one basket, and I don't have a backup plan at this point."

"There's always Ohio," she says and gives an exaggerated shiver.

"My thought exactly. Although I'd really like to be in the same city as Derrick, I have zero interest in Ohio. I got enough of the cold muck in Chicago for the last four years. I know it gets cold and snowy here in Poplar Falls, but that weather is a whole different level of miserable."

"I'm sure it will all work out just like it's meant to. God has a plan and all. Jeez, I'm starting to sound like Doreen, aren't I?" She rolls her eyes.

"A little bit," I agree on a laugh.

We hear tiny feet pounding down the staircase as Beau comes carrying a large duffel bag over his shoulder and a child-sized rod in his hand.

"I'm ready, Auntie Bells," he says as he heaves the bag onto the floor at the door. He bounces over to kiss his momma and sister good night.

"You be good for Beverly and Winston tonight, okay? Go to bed without whining and make sure you brush your teeth first," Dallas instructs.

"Yes, ma'am." He hops up onto the sofa beside them and wraps his arms around her shoulders. "I'm going to miss you," he tells her, and I see her begin to tear up.

"We'll miss you too. Who's Mommy's favorite boy in the whole wide world?"

"Me!"

"That's right, baby."

He releases her and looks to me.

"Are you ready?" he asks impatiently.

Knowing that's my cue, I stand up. "Dude, I've been waiting on you forever. Of course I'm ready!"

Myer walks us out to my car, which already has the top lowered, and he straps Beau's booster chair into my backseat. Once he has his son secured, we pull out and head to scoop up Elle.

"You need a car," I tell Elle something she already knows as she gets into the Mustang with us.

"Why? Between you, Sonia, and Walker, I have a ride everywhere I want to go, and I don't have to worry about pumping gas or paying insurance."

I hear a snicker from the back and look at Beau in the rearview mirror.

"What's so funny?" I ask him.

"She got you there," he says.

"Well, I won't be here much longer. You'll be down one chauffeur in a couple of months," I tell her.

"Don't leave us, Auntie Bells," Beau pleads.

"Oh, Beau, I won't be far. Just a few hours' drive away. I promise I'll come see you and Faith every chance I get."

"But you can stay here, like Miss Sophie did. All you have to do is get Mr. Braxton to build you your own house," he helpfully informs me.

"Is that all?"

"Yep." He nods.

"I'll have to talk to him about that, then."

"He'll do it for you because you are nice and pretty, like Miss Sophie. He likes nice, pretty girls," he tells us.

"What man doesn't?" Elle mumbles under her breath.

When we pull up to Walker's shack, the driveway is packed with vehicles.

"I didn't know he had a full house this evening," I say as I park next to Payne's truck.

"Yeah, he's recruiting all the help he can get. He's so anxious to get it finished," she tells me as I pick Beau up out of the back and stand him on his feet.

An old hound dog comes around the house, barking.

"Hush, Woof. It's just me," Elle calls to him, and he stands and waits as Beau scurries to him.

"Hey, Woof," he says as he scratches the dog behind the ears.

The two of them mosey around the side of the house, and we follow.

The back is full of activity. Pop—Sophie's grandfather—and Jefferson are standing at an old saw table, cutting what looks like well-worn wood. Braxton and Payne are up on scaffolding, trimming the roof, and Walker and Silas are carrying two large iron rails from the back of Walk's pickup to the front opening of the massive barn.

"Wow, you weren't kidding. He is literally turning a barn into a house," I say in awe.

"Isn't it cool as shit?" she asks as she beams up at it. "Come on. I'll show you the inside," she says, and I follow her up to the front of the construction.

"Hey, babe," she says as she smacks Walker on the ass when we pass him.

"Hey now. I'm not a piece of meat, woman," he says in mock offense.

She stops, turns, and gives him a kiss on the cheek.

"That's more like it."

"What about you, Bells? Give me some sugar," he says as he leans his cheek to me.

"Eww," I say as I push him away.

"I'll give you sugar, Walker," Beau says as he stomps up beside us.

"You save your sugar for the ladies, little man. Give me some skin," Walker tells him as he extends his hand out.

Beau grins and slaps it as hard as he can.

I put my hand to Beau's back and lead him into the barn with Elle and me, so he doesn't get in the way of any of the adults' work.

"Whoa, look at that!" Beau says as we step inside.

He runs to the right and looks into the room with an open door.

"This place is amazing, Elle, even better than you described it," I marvel as I take in the massive space.

Pop Lancaster and Jefferson carry in the reclaimed wood door they created and attach it to the track above one of the rows of stalls that lines the far wall. Each stall has a bed inside.

"I can't believe they are so far along." I'm amazed at the progress they've made in a few short months.

"Braxton and Walker are on a mission to get it finished before Sophie delivers," she says.

"When are you planning to move in?"

"I plan to move in next year, after the wedding. Walker could move on in if he wanted to, but he swears he's happy in the shack until we can move in together."

"I'm surprised you're waiting. I'd want to move right in."

She shrugs. "I don't know. I know it sounds old-fashioned, but on my wedding day, I want to be carried over the threshold into our new home as man and wife. Besides, it will probably take that long to get all the final touches and the decorating done, and I don't want to move in until it all comes together."

That's our Elle, always the rule follower. Even in high school. While Sonia and I were rebelling and misbehaving, she was the steadfast one, constantly trying to keep us in check. Though we managed to drag her into a few of our schemes from time to time.

"Can this one be my room?" Beau asks as he rolls open the door Jefferson just finished hanging.

"It sure can. I'll even have Walker put your name on the door," Elle offers.

"Cool!"

We make our way out to the patio on the back of the house, which already has a big L-shaped outdoor sofa surrounding a rock firepit. We sit and can hear the nearby stream trickling behind the trees. We chat and wait for the fellas to finish their work for the day.

Once they are done, Walker comes and squats down beside Elle.

"You finished?"

"For the day, yes."

"I'll go grab us some towels and a cooler," she says before walking to the shack.

Beau and Woof come running up.

"Hey, little man. You ready to go play in some wet water?" Walker asks him.

Beau gives him a funny look.

"Did you just say, 'wet water'?" I ask.

"Yep."

"You're a dipshit."

Elle walks up.

"Woman, your friend is calling me names again."

"What did you call him, Bells?"

"A dipshit."

She purses her lips and thinks for a moment. Then, she shrugs. "I'll allow it."

Beau snickers.

"Hey, you're supposed to be on my side," Walker says as he picks Beau up and tosses him over his shoulder.

Woof starts barking up at him.

"You too, dog. You're both traitors."

Walker leads us to his pier, and he takes Elle, Beau, and me out on his granddaddy's old fishing boat. We spend the rest of the evening out on the "wet water."

Ten

BRANDT

I DRIVE MOM INTO DENVER TO CATCH HER FLIGHT TO PORTLAND.

"There are leftovers in the freezer. I labeled them all and left instructions on how long to heat them. There should be enough to get you through the first week. After that, you'll have to stop and get takeout," she says as I pull her bag from the back of my vehicle.

"Don't worry. I promise I won't starve. I can feed myself, you know," I tell her as I kiss her cheek.

"Lou-Lou's special food is in the refrigerator in the bottom drawer. I give her a small bowl twice a day. First thing when we get up in the morning and then again around five. She's not used to being alone at night, so she may want to sleep in your room. Just pull her bed in and she'll curl up on it. If she gets too anxious, you can call and I'll talk to her over the phone and try to soothe her."

"Vet here, remember? I think I can handle your pup's needs," I mutter.

"That reminds me, Bellamy will be at the clinic first thing Monday morning. I already went over your schedule with her, and she has my number, so she can call me with any questions." She ignores me and continues to fret over her instructions.

"Mom, we'll be fine. It's for two weeks. Nothing is going to fall apart in two weeks. Not me and not the clinic. Just go and enjoy Debbie and the kids," I try to reassure her.

She hugs me tight. "I will, son. I'll miss you though."

"I'll miss you too, Mom."

Once I see her safely into the terminal, I head back home. Home. Poplar Falls is finally starting to feel like home. That is something I never thought would happen when we landed here.

Today, a new tractor is being delivered, so I can start clearing my land, and I have a general contractor coming out at two o'clock to give me a quote on the renovations I have planned for the house. Once the house is complete, I'll start the landscaping.

Since it was built in the 1800s, I was able to go to the Poplar Falls Historical Society office, which is basically a room the size of a large closet off the library downtown, and I had them look up the original blueprints of the house. My goal is to restore it to its former glory but with a few modern upgrades, if at all possible.

I'm not handy myself per se. My father was a businessman, and he taught me a lot about finance and business but not my way around a hammer and chain saw. However, I would love to learn as much as possible and do what work I can with my own two hands. I just need someone with the patience to show me as they go, but the yard I can do. I worked endlessly on ours back in Portland. I was in a non-verbal battle of wills against one of the retired gentlemen down the street on who would have the best manicured lawn. He won, but I gave it my all, and I enjoyed getting my hands in the dirt.

Yesterday I dropped a small fortune on tools at the hardware store and then proceeded to spend the next few hours watching YouTube videos on how to demo a kitchen and how to lay new hardwood floors. They made it look so easy. How hard can it be?

Eleven

BELLAMY

I ARRIVE EARLY FOR MY FIRST DAY OF WORK AT THE CLINIC. I WASN'T exactly sure how to dress, so I decided on a pair of wide-leg soft-gray linen dress pants, an off-the-shoulder white drop blouse with a darker gray satin ribbon across the top, and a pair of pencil-strap black stilettos. I let my hair fall in beach waves and did my makeup for the first time this summer. I assess my reflection in the glass door before I enter, and I like the look. As much as I enjoy the laid-back, natural lifestyle on the ranch, every woman loves a reason to get gussied up from time to time.

The bell above the door chimes as I enter the front office.

I drop my purse behind the sleek black desk and head down the hallway to start the coffeepot.

As I turn the corner to the small break room, a door opens. Dr. Haralson steps out in my path, and we collide.

"Whoa," he says as he clutches my bare shoulder to steady me as I lose my balance.

"Sorry," I offer. "I guess I'm out of practice, walking in heels."

He looks down at my feet and then slowly raises his gaze back up my body.

"You look very nice," he chokes out.

"I bet I smell better than I did, covered in horse afterbirth too," I tease.

He leans in and inhales deeply.

"So much better," he agrees.

When he lets me go, I walk into the break room, and he follows with Lou-Lou on his heels.

"Is there anything you need me to do at the moment? I was about to start the coffee and then take a look at the schedule for today."

"Could you call out to Rustic Peak and ask Braxton if we can reschedule my visit this afternoon for some time next week? I have a load of lumber being dropped off at my house, and I'd like to be there, if at all possible," he says as he opens the cabinet above the sink and hands me a bag of ground coffee.

I wrinkle my nose at the offered sack.

"What?" he asks.

"You drink that stuff?"

He looks down at the bag in his hand, confused. "Yes."

"Gross. I'll pop into Dallas's shop and grab us a couple of to-go cups, and then at lunch, I'll walk down to the market and get some quality coffee to brew for tomorrow."

"Seriously? You can make this for me and get something else for yourself, if you'd like," he says as he tries to hand it over.

"No way. You're not drinking that either. Now, go to your office and do whatever you need to get ready for the day, and I'll be back before we open."

I shoo him toward the door, and he shakes his head like I'm crazy.

"All right, I know better than to argue with a woman." He gives in.

"Smart man," I call after him.

I hear a yap and look down to see Lou-Lou watching me with anticipation.

"Come on, girl, let's go for a walk and get Doc some decent java to kick-start his day."

When we make it over to Bountiful Harvest, Doreen is sitting at a table, chatting with Dottie, who is icing cupcakes behind the counter.

"Good morning, ladies," I greet as Lou-Lou noses past me and bounces over to sit in front of the counter awaiting one of the treats Dottie always keeps for the fur babies that come in with her customers.

"Bellamy, don't you look spiffy this morning?" Doreen says, and I do a turn.

"Why, thank you, ma'am," I say while doing a little curtsy.

"What's the occasion?" she asks.

"I'm filling in for Miss Elaine over at the vet clinic for a couple of weeks while she visits with her grandchildren. I just wanted to look professional," I explain.

She gives me a conspiratorial look. "That Dr. Brandt isn't hard on the eyes, is he?"

"He sure isn't, but this is a strictly professional relationship," I say pointedly.

"You never know. Love grows in unexpected places," she says more to herself than to me.

"No, I do know. According to Elle, Doc prefers his single status, and I'm not going to be here much longer anyway. Hopefully."

"I'm not so sure Brandt prefers it as much as he is trapped in it," she says cryptically. "And the quickest way to make God laugh is to tell him your plans, young lady."

I sit in the seat beside her. "Don't go throwing all that wise, old logic and voodoo you do all over me, Aunt Doreen," I playfully command.

"No voodoo about it. And if you live long enough, you'll understand one day when Beau and Faith are stumbling around, trying to find their way. A little nudge in the right direction from Auntie Bells might be just what they need."

Hmm ... I like the thought of that.

"Can I get you anything, dear?" Dottie asks as she takes the tray of fresh cupcakes and places it in the clear display case before tossing Lou-Lou a biscuit.

"Oh, yes, I forgot. Two large coffees with cream, one with two sugars, and toss in a couple of those banana nut muffins, please."

I open my purse to grab my wallet just as my phone starts to vibrate.

I pull it out and read the display to see that the call is coming in from Denver.

I call to Dottie that I'll be right back and excuse myself, stepping outside as I answer the call.

"This is Bellamy Wilson," I greet the caller.

"Miss Wilson, this is Cathy with Dr. Singh's office at the Denver Zoo," she begins.

My stomach does a little flip. *This is it.*

"It's nice to speak to you, Cathy. I hope you are having a good morning."

"Yes, I am, and I wish I were calling under better circumstances. Dr. Singh wanted me to let you know that, unfortunately, he had to make the difficult decision to go with a different candidate for the animal nutritionist position. He was very impressed by your résumé, and all of your references spoke highly of you, including our own staff that you worked with here at the zoo, but after careful consideration, another applicant has been offered the job."

"I see," I whisper as I try to hold off the sob that is forming in the back of my throat.

"Bellamy, Dr. Singh wanted me to let you know that you were the other applicant in the running, and you were barely nudged out by someone more qualified. He plans to keep your résumé on file, and if any new positions come open within the department, you will be first in line," she consoles.

"Please tell Dr. Singh thank you for me," I manage to say.

"I will, and you be patient. I'm sure you'll be a part of the Denver Zoo family in the near future."

I end the call and stare at the phone in my hand for a long while.

Dottie sticks her head out of the door and calls to me, "Your coffees are going to get cold, dear."

"Oh, of course. I'll be right there."

I compose myself and plant a smile on my face before I go in to claim and pay for my order.

Then, gather my purchase and Lou-Lou, bid good-bye to the ladies and stroll back to the clinic, lost in my thoughts.

What do I do now? I didn't have a plan B.

Twelve

BELLAMY

I TRIED TO PUT MY DISAPPOINTMENT IN THE BACK OF MY MIND AND give the day my full attention. The clinic was busy from the moment I flipped the Open sign until an hour past closing. Brandt saw steady patients at the office and made four big-animal house calls in between. Everyone was very patient as they waited for his return, but it was chaotic at best.

After the last family leaves with their newly neutered pup, I lock the door and begin to close out the computer for the night.

"Thank you for all the help today, Bellamy. You probably weren't expecting to be a secretary, babysitter, dog sitter, clinical assistant, and housekeeper, all at once."

I look from the screen to Brandt, who is leaning against the door-frame, watching me.

"It was fine. I like a quick-paced job. Besides, being busy makes the day go faster and keeps me out of my own head," I tell him.

He considers me for a moment and nods. "I agree."

He turns to head back to his office, and I stop him.

"Can I ask you a question?"

He looks back at me.

"Is it always like this? Because if it is, you obviously need some real help. It might be time for Poplar Falls to look into getting a do-mestic/family-animal vet in addition to a large-animal vet. I know Dr. Sherrill handled it all himself for many years, but the town is growing, and so are the ranches. It might be more than one man can handle before too long."

He sighs. "To be honest, I've put some feelers out for a vet tech. The practice can afford a decent salary, and there is a lot a technician can do that wouldn't require my personal attention, which would free me up for house calls quite a bit. They could handle the routine exams and vaccinations while I was out of the office, and they could assist me in surgery, which would make those go quicker. They could even assist me out in the field when needed.

"I'd love to free Mom up from some of the workload she takes on. I know she enjoys working, but I think she'd prefer to go to part-time hours and be semi-retired. The problem is, there aren't any locals with the education and skill set we need, and I haven't come across anyone online, looking to relocate to Colorado, but I'll keep trying. Until then, we just have to make it work," he confides.

"I'll be happy to do some searching on your behalf as well. Maybe some of my college friends or sorority sisters know of someone who could be interested," I offer.

"I'd appreciate that."

"You got it, Doc," I say as I finish up and gather my things.

"Would you like to go to dinner with me?"

"Dinner?" I ask, surprised by his request.

"Yes, to thank you for the hard day's work and to apologize for the hard day's work," he explains.

I consider him for a moment. He looks expectant. I assume he doesn't have a lot of friends in town, and no one likes to eat alone.

"Sure, I'll just call Momma and tell her not to expect me tonight," I accept.

"Great. Let me finish up a few things, and we'll head to the diner. It's meatloaf night," he says with a wag of his eyebrows.

I call Momma, who doesn't seem the least bit upset that I'm skipping out on her tonight, and then I type a quick text to Derrick while I wait for Brandt.

I didn't get the job. :(

Ugh, maybe I'll end up taking him up on his offer for a job at Columbus. Ohio might not be so bad. I should give it a chance. Doreen could be right after all, and the Lord is just giving me a push in a different direction for my own good. I have to go with the flow and see where it leads me.

I put my phone away and decide to enjoy the rest of my evening and not think about what's next. Worrying myself sick isn't going to change a thing anyway.

We decide to walk to Faye's Diner since it's such a nice night.

"You mentioned a delivery to a house earlier. Are you moving?" I make small talk as we stroll.

"Not yet. I purchased the property for sale at the end of Mashstomp Road, and I'm going to renovate it. It'll be a while before it's move-in ready, I'm afraid."

I stop dead. He realizes this, and he halts and turns to look at me. His eyebrows rise in question.

"Wait, are you telling me you bought the old Sugarman Homestead?" I ask.

"I did," he answers.

"Oh my goodness, are you serious?" I squeal. "Do you know that place has been abandoned since we were little? Sonia, Elle, and I used to dream of buying it one day, and the three of us were going to live in it and raise our families in it, like an old, Southern *Dynasty* or something. Each of us with our own wing. We planned to throw posh parties and holiday balls like they did in Elizabethan London and live like high-society lords and ladies," I tell him in my best British accent as I twirl.

His eyes alight with humor.

"I shall make sure I have a ballroom added, then, just for you ladies," he playfully agrees.

"You have to take me to see it! We've only ever gotten a glimpse from the windows, and I've been dying to see the inside all these years.

"The Sugarmans were one of the original families who founded Poplar Falls. Mr. Sugarman built that house as a wedding gift to his bride. He spent two years here, overseeing its construction before he brought her, their teenage son, and twin daughters down from Colorado Springs. It was a grand monument to his love."

"How romantic," he muses.

"Isn't it? Sad that he lost his wife and daughters to a fever five years later. Once their son grew up and moved to California, he lived in that big, old house alone. After his death, his son sold the house to a developer who planned to tear it down and use the land for planting, but the town had it declared a historical landmark, and he couldn't demo it, so he let it sit there and rot. Eventually, the bank foreclosed on the property. It's been vacant ever since. I sure am glad someone finally saw its potential," I tell him.

We make it to Faye's, and the place is slammed. Meatloaf night is a big one around here. No one does it better than her cook, Andy.

We chat as we enjoy our meal. Dr. Brandt is as intelligent and witty as he is handsome. He regales me with stories from his college days and a few of his more memorable experiences as a vet. I'm pleased that our adventure with the birth of little Ali makes the top ten.

When we finish, he walks me back to the Mustang parked out front of the clinic.

"Thank you again for today," he says as I climb behind the wheel. "And you were right about the coffee. I had no idea what we were missing."

"Life's too short to drink shoddy java, Doc."

"That it is," he agrees.

I turn the ignition.

"See you tomorrow," I say with a wave.

He returns my wave and stands and watches until I drive out of sight. *What a pleasant evening it turned out to be.*

Halfway home, my phone starts to ring.

"Hello?"

"Hey, babe," Derrick says.

"Hey," I say.

"I'm sorry about the job," he starts.

I sigh. "Me too. I guess it just wasn't meant to be."

"So, you're not mad?" he asks cautiously.

"I guess not, disappointed maybe," I admit.

"I want you to know I wasn't expecting it. Dr. Singh and I just started communicating, and one thing led to another. This is actually a good thing, if you think about it. I'll go ahead and find an apartment and once I'm settled you can move in. Then, as soon as something becomes available, I can get you in at the zoo, and our logistics problem is solved. So, if you look at it that way, it's actually the best-case scenario."

I'm not really following.

"Wait, I thought you were going to stay in your parents' basement for now?" I ask, confused.

The line goes silent.

"Derrick? Are you still there?"

I look down at my phone to make sure I haven't lost the signal.

"Hello?" I try again.

"They didn't tell you?" he asks.

"Tell me what?"

"Dr. Singh offered me the job at the Denver Zoo, and I accepted the position this afternoon. I start the week after my master's program is completed."

What?

"What job?" I ask.

"Animal nutritionist."

He gives me a moment while the news sinks in.

"Bellamy?"

"You stole my job?" I ask slowly, hoping I heard him wrong.

"It wasn't like that," he begins to explain.

"It is exactly like that," I scream into the phone.

"Sweetheart, listen to me."

"Go to hell, Derrick!"

I hit the button to end the call. I get a notification of an incoming text from him moments later.

Bellamy, we need to talk. I know it was a shock, but it will be great for our future. I'll be able to lay the groundwork and build a foundation for you, for us. Then, you'll be working in Denver, like you always dreamed. It'll happen soon, and you'll be by my side. Sleep on it, and we'll talk tomorrow. I miss you.

He has got to be kidding me.

I press the side button to turn the phone off.

What a jackass.

Thirteen

BELLAMY

I BARELY SLEPT A WINK. I TOSSED AND TURNED AND STEWED IN MY anger all night long.

When I make it to the kitchen in the morning, Myer is standing at the island with Momma.

I plop into a stool and drop my head onto my folded arm as I mumble, "Coffee."

"What did you get into last night, sis?" Myer asks as I hear Momma open the cabinet to grab me a mug.

"Nothing. I just couldn't sleep."

Not buying it, Momma slides a mug of coffee in front of me and asks, "What's the matter, Bells?"

I lift my head and look at her. There's no use evading. She's always been able to read me like a book.

"I didn't get the job at the zoo," I say.

"Oh, honey, I'm so sorry," she starts.

"It gets worse," I tell her. "Derrick got the job. The one he hadn't even applied for. The one he'd only known about and contacted the doctor about to give a reference for me!"

"Derrick? Are you serious?" she bites.

I nod.

"That ... that ... rat!" she exclaims.

I nod again.

"And get this: he thinks I should be happy about it. That I should move in with him and wait patiently while he works out a place for me at the zoo," I tell them.

"He has gone and lost his mind," Momma declares.

"Yep, I can't believe it. I thought I had this job in the bag. I know Dr. Singh thought I was good. I guess just not good enough."

"Not good enough? Are you serious? I wish you'd strike that phrase from your vocabulary young lady," she scolds.

"It's true, Momma."

"No, it's not! It's just something you go around saying too often: How much time do you have? Not enough. How much sleep did you get last night? Not enough. You look amazing, how much weight have you lost? Not enough. How much money do you make? Not enough. You use it so much that you have started to believe it about yourself, but you hear me Bellamy Wilson, you are fearfully and wonderfully made, and you are more than enough. Do you understand me?"

My lips begin to tremble at her declaration and I look up and nod my head in agreement.

"Thank you, Momma," I whisper.

She places her hand on my cheek and squeezes. "Don't you worry, Bells. You can stay right here until you figure out your next move. And don't you settle either. You will find something just as good or even better. When God closes one door, he opens an even better one. You just have to be patient and willing to trust Him and walk through it when the time comes."

I grip her arm and lean into her hand.

"Now, let's make you some breakfast. Chocolate chip pancakes are great at healing the soul," she offers.

"Thanks, Momma, but I have to get a shower and get to the clinic. We have a busy day today."

I take one last sip of the coffee and then push back from the island and stand.

Myer doesn't say anything. He simply envelops me in his massive arms for a few seconds. He doesn't need words. I just absorb my big brother's love and support.

Then, he releases me, and I head upstairs to get my day started.

Today is busier than yesterday. I'm not sure how that is even possible, but it is definitely welcome. I don't have the time to dwell on my career status, and I keep my phone off all day, effectively avoiding Derrick and his flimsy excuses and apologies.

Once we close up for the day, Brandt asks if I have plans for supper again.

"Another date, Doc? The town is going to start whispering. I bet you and I were already the hot topic of the day at Janelle's salon," I tease.

He looks confused for a moment, and it's absolutely adorable.

"No, I mean, I was going to ride out to the house and thought you might want to come along."

"Yes! I'd love to," I accept immediately.

"There isn't any electricity on there yet, but there is running water, so we can stop for takeout and eat there, if you're hungry," he offers.

"I'll call us in a sandwich order to Dottie. What would you like?" I ask as I pick up the phone and dial.

"Surprise me," he says and then disappears down the hallway.

"This place is just as magical as I imagined it would be," I say as we walk around the first floor.

Two large, hand-carved wooden doors open up to a grand foyer. A split ivory staircase with an intricate mahogany banister winding down both sides leads up to the second floor. To the right is a huge living room with an old piano in front of the bay windows that overlook the overgrown front lawn. The left leads to a parlor with a fireplace on one wall, and it sides up to the kitchen.

"There are five bedrooms and three baths upstairs and a small room off the kitchen behind the stairs, which I think might have been for the cook or maybe the maid's quarters at one time. My plan is to gut the kitchen and completely remodel it. I want to remove this wall and turn the parlor into a dining room that opens to the living room. I'll restore the staircase and refinish all the wood. Sand and keep all the original floors. The largest room upstairs, I'm going to turn into a master suite and expand the attached bath and add two walk-in closets. That will take one of the smaller bedrooms, and it will end up as a four-bedroom home instead of five."

As he explains his home plans, I can envision exactly what it will look like, and it sounds amazing.

I walk over to the stairs and run my hands along the banister. "It's going to be spectacular. The mix of the new and the old world. The bones are lovely, and adding the modern touches is going to make it something special," I tell him.

"Yeah, that's what I thought too," he agrees.

"May I?" I ask as I gesture up to the second floor.

"Please." He extends his arm in invitation, and I make my way to the top.

I walk the circular, open layout, peeking into each room. They are very Victorian and nothing that I imagine Brandt would like.

"I'll update these too. Bigger closets, fresh paint, and new furniture," he says.

"I'm jealous," I declare as we make it back to the staircase. "I do believe you are going to have a dream home when you finish."

He looks around. "If I ever finish. It's not like I have tons of free time lying around. But it'll be a fun project. I'm looking forward to the work. Come on. You haven't seen the best part." He beckons, and

I follow him out the back door and onto a concrete veranda that over-looks the yard.

"Wow," is all I manage to get out as I take in the back side of the property. It's better than I remember. So tranquil.

It's hidden from the road, and I never realized how massive the land back here was.

"I thought maybe I'd have a pool put in," he starts.

I vaguely remember this place being abloom with color.

"Are you kidding? This is meant to be a garden. One of those that has pathways and benches for meditation and reflection. A place for picnics and barbecues. You don't want to ruin it with a pool that you can only open a couple of months a year. Besides, I bet the river is just beyond that tree line." I point toward the wooded area off in the distance. "You can swim out there whenever you want."

He considers me for a moment, and then he looks out over the space. I can see his mind working behind his eyes.

"A garden," he repeats.

"A magnificent garden full of beautiful blooms and fruit trees and a gazebo," I suggest.

"And a she-shed for Mom, one that looks like a cottage, there in that corner by the fountain." He gestures toward the far right.

"I imagine she'd love it," I utter. "Sounds perfect."

"It does," he agrees.

"What's that?" I point toward a stack of lumber to the side of the patio.

"Building material. I had it delivered. I bought a tractor to start clearing the land, and I need a utility shed or garage to keep it in."

"You planning to build a garage yourself?"

"No, ma'am. I plan to hire a contractor to build me one."

"Foster is a master carpenter. He helped Myer build his cabin. I bet he'd be willing to do a side job, if you are okay with him working after hours. He does good work," I recommend.

"Foster. Thank you for the tip. I'll talk to him tomorrow."

I look back at the house and then turn to him in question. "You wouldn't happen to need any help demoing the kitchen, would you?"

He considers me.

"I guess another set of hands couldn't hurt anything. Why?" he asks.

I shrug. "I feel like tearing some shit up."

Fourteen

BRANDT

I HAND HER A PAIR OF GOGGLES, NOT SURE HOW I GOT TALKED INTO this.

"I wasn't exactly planning to start on this tonight," I tell her.

"Why wait?" she says as she looks at the tools I have laid out before us.

"Because I haven't had a professional come in to tell me where the plumbing and wiring are located and which walls are load-bearing. We could potentially cave the whole house in," I inform her.

"Oh, we won't do all of that. Don't be a drama queen," she says as she rolls her eyes. "We'll just pull off the cabinet doors and bust out the drawers for now."

She chooses a crowbar and starts on the doors.

I watch as she takes her aggression out on the first one. And then the next. She goes down the line and uses the crowbar like a bat to knock each one from its hinges. By the time she gets to the last one, her face is red, and she has tears streaming down her cheeks.

She turns to the bottom set of cabinets, and before she can swing, I grab the crowbar from her and she looks up at me in surprise.

"Want to talk about it?" I ask.

She slides her eyes to the side. "Not really," she whispers.

"I'm a good listener," I prompt.

"I hate him. He really cranks my tractor," she says as she swipes under her eyes.

"He?" I ask.

"Derrick. My 'boyfriend.' " She throws her hands up and uses air quotes on the word *boyfriend* and continues without taking a breath, "*It will be great for our future. I'm laying the groundwork, building a foundation here for you and me.* Who the hell does he think he is?"

"The one who cranks your tractor?" I ask.

"Yes, he cranks my tractor!" she screams.

I put my hands up and watch as she kicks the busted doors into a pile.

"I worked my ass off, preparing for that position. I interned for the department head the summer before last, and he said I did an excellent job. I pledged his prissy little granddaughter's sorority. I even changed my minor at his suggestion. I graduated with honors, for goodness' sake. And Dr. Singh goes and gives the job to Derrick?"

"Derrick, your boyfriend," I state, trying to keep up.

"Ex-boyfriend—sort of. He was someone I was seeing back in Chicago. It wasn't super serious or anything, not yet. Anyway, he was an assistant to my biochem professor. I used him as a reference on my résumé and asked him to give a recommendation for me. And the rat bastard snaked the job right out from under me. Can you believe that?"

"Did he know it was so important to you?"

"Of course he knew! He already had a job waiting for him in Ohio, and he begged me to come with him and take an assistant job. But I didn't want that. I wanted to work in Denver, and I wanted that animal nutritionist job. He knew that. I love working with animals. He had no interest in it. He had a guaranteed job, and he took mine. And he has the nerve to say he did it for me."

She stops her tirade to look at me.

"Why do men do that? Do you think we're stupid?" she asks me.

"Um …" I start.

"Like, do you really think that making decisions for us is going to make us happy?"

"I don't think—"

"He even said he was apartment-hunting for us. *Us.* As if I would come running straight to him when I found out the good news."

I carefully approach her and whisper, "I'm sorry, Bellamy."

"He ruined everything." She sniffles.

"I know. I know you're disappointed, but you are smart and talented, and you are going to have your pick of jobs," I tell her.

"I wanted that one," she grumbles.

"Maybe it just wasn't the one for you. The job or the guy," I console.

She laughs. "You think?"

"Probably not," I say, and she finally grants me a grin.

She sighs.

"At least Beau is going to be thrilled now that I'll be in Poplar Falls a little longer."

"I think you'll find a lot of people will be happy now that you'll be around a bit longer."

She blinks up at me. "Yeah?"

"Yeah."

She laughs. "Jeez, I'm a mess. I'm sorry about the mini breakdown. We barely know each other, and I'm laying all my shit on you. How embarrassing." She looks me in the eye. "I guess we're friends now, Doc. No going back now."

"Lucky me," I say as I wrap my arm around her neck and lead her away from the kitchen. "Come on. We're running out of light, and I still need to feed you."

I start my vehicle and turn the headlights on. Bellamy is sitting on the stoop with our supper spread out in front of her. The light catches her profile, and she turns toward it. When it illuminates her face, I'm taken aback by how beautiful she truly is.

She's the exact opposite of Annie in every way. Annie had straight, shoulder-length, dark hair and big brown eyes. She was petite and had an olive complexion. Bellamy is tall and lean with milky skin and long blonde hair, which has a natural wave, and gorgeous deep blue eyes. Different but both beautiful.

Why am I comparing her to Annie?

I sit there, trying to sort my head when I hear my name.

"Brandt? Are you joining me or what?" Bellamy asks as she shields her eyes from the light.

I leave all my thoughts of Annie in the cab, and I step out and make my way to Bellamy.

"Your feast, good sir," she says as she gestures to the sandwich and chips.

My stomach growls, and she smiles up at me.

"Ah, looks like we're just in time."

I sit beside her, and she extends a sandwich in my direction.

"Chicken salad. It's Dottie's specialty."

I lean in and take a huge bite of the offered food.

She raises an eyebrow and waits.

"Mmm, that's good," I say, and I take another bite before she has a chance to pull it back.

"Told you so," she brags.

"Can I ask you something?"

"Sure," she says as she takes a bite herself.

"Are you more upset over losing the job or the boyfriend?"

She thinks for a moment while she chews.

"The job," she admits.

I smile at her. "Good."

"Why is that?" she asks.

"Because broken plans are a lot easier to recover from than a broken heart."

Her eyes meet mine, and understanding passes between us. Or maybe it's just my imagination.

"Today was fun. You know, I really would love to help you work on this house. I mean, I can't build walls or anything, but I can sand floors, and I'm pretty good with a paintbrush. And it just so happens that I have a lot of free time on my hands all of a sudden." She looks at me with hope-filled eyes.

"I'm not about to turn down an offer for free labor, although I doubt you'll be able to top your talent with a crowbar, Miss Wilson."

"You just wait," she says before she pops a chip in her mouth. "I have talent you haven't even begun to tap into yet, Doc."

Oh, I have no doubt.

Fifteen

BELLAMY

"THANK YOU, BELLAMY," MR. HINSON SAYS AS I HAND HIM his receipt.

"You're welcome. And remember, Odie needs to wear that cone until you bring him back to have those sutures removed," I instruct.

"He's going to hate that."

"I know, but you have to be strong," I tell him.

The bell rings, and I look past the two to see Elle breeze in.

"Hi, Bells, Mr. Hinson," she greets.

"Elle, how are you, gorgeous?" Mr. Hinson asks.

He's always been an old flirt.

"I'm great. How about you?" she asks.

"Growing old. Trying to stay spry," he says and gives her a gap-toothed smile.

"Oh, fiddlesticks. You're only old when it suits you," I tease him.

"When it gets me a little extra love from a pretty girl," he admits.

She obliges and kisses his cheek.

"Aw, what happened to Odie?" Elle asks him.

"He got after the chickens again. They lit him up." He laughs.

We hear a horn honk outside, and he grumbles.

"I'd best get going. Sounds like the old lady is getting impatient."

He walks out, and Elle turns to me. I look at the clock, and it says ten past noon.

"You're just in time. I'm starving. Let me grab my purse," I tell her.

"Um, I'm sorry, Bells, but I already have lunch plans," she says.

I look up, confused.

"Oh. Why'd you swing by, then?" I ask.

"I have a lunch date with Brandt. I'm just here to meet him."

That gets my attention. I stand and face her.

"A lunch date with Brandt?" I ask.

"Yep," she confirms just as Brandt walks in from the back of the office.

"I thought I heard your voice. Give me just a minute, and I'll be ready," he tells her, and she nods.

He smiles at us both before walking back to his office.

"So, where are you two going?" I ask casually.

"I'm not sure where he's taking me. Probably over to the café. It's chili day, and he is a creature of habit," she says.

"Do you guys have lunch together often?"

"Every now and then. Why?"

"Walker okay with that?" I ask curiously, and she smiles.

"Walker doesn't have a problem with Brandt. He knows we're friends."

That surprises me. Elle and Brandt dated briefly last year before she and Walker realized they had feelings for each other.

"If you say so," I mumble. "See you later. Enjoy lunch."

I throw my purse over my shoulder and make for the door. She steps in front of me.

"Just a minute. What was that all about?" She raises an eyebrow at me in question.

"Nothing. Walker just seems like the jealous type, so it surprises me that you and Brandt have lunch together; that's all. But if it's not an issue, then it's not an issue."

"Uh-huh," she says, unconvinced.

"I'm serious. I was just looking out for you."

"Walker knows I'm not going anywhere. His ring is on my finger, and for some reason, I'm crazy about the man. Brandt and I are friends. Walker doesn't dictate my friends. You know that."

"Would you feel the same if he were taking a female friend to lunch?" I ask.

"Of course. He takes Sonia to lunch all the time, so they can discuss his mother's care. What's going on with you?"

"Ugh, I don't know. I've had a rough couple of days, and I haven't had a chance to fill you in," I confess.

"Why didn't you just say that? Do you want me to cancel with Brandt? We can go grab a bite and talk if you need to."

"No, don't do that. I don't want to ruin your plans. I'm sorry. I have to run out to the house anyway."

"Walker wants to go out tonight. Some band he likes is playing at Butch's Tavern. Why don't you come too? I'll call Sonia and get her and Ricky to come. We'll have drinks, and you can tell us all about it."

"That sounds good." I give in.

"We'll pick you up, and that way, Walker can drive, so we can drink."

I give her a doubtful look.

"Don't worry. If I'm with him, he makes sure not to have more than two beers."

"What have you done to him, witch?" I tease.

Brandt remerges.

"Ready?" he asks Elle.

"I am."

"I'll see you guys later. Enjoy lunch," I tell them before I walk out and to my car.

I turn the ignition and watch while the two of them chat as he locks the office. Then, she takes his arm, and they walk off toward the café.

I don't like it. And it pisses me off because I have no idea why it bothers me.

I pull up at the house, and Momma is on the porch, holding Faith in her arms.

"What do you have there?" I ask.

"My favorite granddaughter," she coos at the baby. "Beau is out, following Myer around while he works, and Dallas is inside on the couch, napping."

"Good. I'm glad she came over, so she could get some rest."

"Oh, she didn't. She came to drop Beau off, and while she was waiting for Myer to come get him, she sat down with the baby in her arms and fell right off to sleep. I gently took Faith from her, turned off the television, and threw a blanket over her, and Beau and I snuck out as quietly as we could. Faith and I have been sitting here ever since, swinging and enjoying the cool afternoon."

"Bless her heart, I'll just sit here with you two, then, so I don't disturb her."

I take a seat on the swing and open my arms.

Momma reluctantly gives up the sleeping baby.

"That boy has called the house a dozen times today," she tells me.

I roll my eyes. "Ignore him," I tell her.

"Bellamy, you can't avoid him forever."

"Sure I can."

"An adult would call him back and end things properly," she scolds.

"An adult would have told me he decided to steal the job right out from under me. No, actually, an adult wouldn't have taken the job in the first place."

She sighs.

"That's true enough," she agrees.

"He'll figure it out and stop calling soon, Momma. I have no desire to hash anything out with him."

"Okay, sweetheart. But I can't promise that your father won't have an earful for him if he answers and Derrick is on the line."

I shrug. That's a chance he takes.

The baby shifts in my arms, opens her eyes, and lets out a loud cry. I shush her and try to rock her back to sleep, but she is not having it.

"Faith!"

We hear the panicked call from inside.

"She's out here, Dallas," Momma calls to her.

A disheveled Dallas emerges from the house.

"Is she okay?" she asks.

"Just fine. Apparently, it's lunchtime though," I say as I nod to her.

Dallas looks down at her T-shirt. The telltale signs of a leaky boob show.

"Yep, the milk factory is full. Give me," she says as she reaches for the baby.

"I wish I could feed her for you," I say as I pass her off.

"I'll switch her to a bottle when I go back to work in a few weeks, but I want to breastfeed her for as long as I can. I know I look a hot mess, but I really enjoy it."

"You look wonderful," Momma insists.

Dallas shakes her head.

"You do, Dal. You are glowing," I agree.

"Thank you. And thanks for the power nap. I feel much better."

"You can come here to nap anytime," Momma says before standing. "I'm getting hungry myself. I think I'll go rustle up some lunch for the three of us too," she announces before walking inside.

"I heard about what your douche-bag man did," Dallas says as soon as the door closes behind her.

"Did Momma tell you?"

"Yeah. She let the phone go to the answering machine a couple of times, and I asked what was going on."

"I'm so angry," I tell her.

"If you want my two cents, I say it's better you know now than waste years of your life with him and then find out that he is a selfish prick. Trust me."

"Honestly, I think I'm relieved. I was counting on the job, but I don't think I ever saw Derrick and me going the distance. I believe he was more serious about us than I was. I'm more pissed that, now, if I do end up in Denver, he'll be there."

She laughs. "Look at it this way: you could always end up as his boss one day and fire his ass," she says with a gleam in her eye.

"I think I just got myself a new goal."

"That's my girl. Don't get mad. Get even."

Sixteen

BRANDT

I WALK INTO BUTCH'S TAVERN AND SEARCH THE CROWD OF FACES, looking for Elle. I have no idea how I let her talk me into this, but she knew Mom was out of town, and I had no excuse as to why I couldn't come out and socialize for a while tonight. Bars aren't usually my thing, but the places here in Poplar Falls are a far cry from the glitzy dance clubs and late-night party scenes my associates used to drag me to in Portland. Here, the atmosphere is laid-back and more of a watering hole for friends to gather together after a hard day's work, like they would at a backyard barbecue.

I spot Walker as he balances a couple of bottles, and I make my way to relieve him of the whiskey glass cradled in the crook of his arm.

"Doc, thanks. Glad you could join us. We're in desperate need of testosterone. All my buddies have been falling off like flies lately. It's just Payne and me left to wrangle a bunch of unruly women by ourselves," Walker greets as he leads me to a large table nestled in the far corner of the space.

"Look who the cat dragged in," Elle squeals as we arrive, and Walker starts distributing beverages.

"This must be yours," I say as I place the glass in front of her.

"Yep, she's my whiskey girl," Walker confirms.

Sonia slides over close to Elle on the bench seat.

"Come on, Doc. We'll make room." She gestures for me to sit beside them.

I look around.

"Where's your husband? I'm sorry. His name escapes me," I ask her.

"Ricky. He is playing poker with some buddies tonight," she says as she rolls her eyes.

I take the offered seat and flag down a waitress. I order a beer and a shot of tequila.

"Now, that's my kind of order," Walker says before raising his beer and taking a long pull.

"I thought you said Bellamy was coming tonight?" I ask Elle.

"She is. Foster is giving her a ride."

Foster.

Elle gives me a curious look and then explains further, "We were going to stop and pick her up, but Walker talked to Foster earlier, and since he wanted to join us and he works out there at Stoney Ridge, it just made sense for him to bring her."

I nod in agreement. "Of course."

I clear my throat and look to the front of the room, where a couple of guys are setting up sound equipment.

"So, you know the band?" I ask Walker.

"Yeah, the drummer is a friend of mine. We used to play in a garage band together in middle school."

"You play?" I ask.

"And he sings." Elle beams. "If we're lucky, we'll be able to get him up there for a song or two tonight."

He grins at her and winks.

Payne joins us, and Walker adds another table to ours and scoots up a few confiscated stools.

Forty-five minutes later, Bellamy breezes in with Foster on her heels.

She has on a beige maxi dress cinched at the waist by a wide braided leather belt with turquoise beads and brown cowgirl boots. Her hair is in a topknot with wisps escaping to frame her face.

Her face alights when she spots our table, and she grabs Foster's hand and leads him over.

My eyes fall to their joined hands as they make it to us.

"Where have you two been?" Elle asks.

"It's his fault. He was in the driveway, talking on the phone forever, while I waited in the truck," Bellamy says as she rounds the table and forces me over with her hip before sitting down.

Foster looks at Walker. "Mom, man. Giving me a hard time. I knew moving back in with her was a bad idea. I have got to get my own place," he says.

"What was she giving you shit about this time?" Walker asks.

"I have no idea. She's been on my ass since the divorce. Today, she was going on about how I've already made one mistake today, and going out tonight would be number two."

"Did you tell her I was going to be here? I don't think she's my biggest fan. I'm working on her though. She'll fall for my charm eventually. They always do." Walker grins at him.

"Yep, she knows, and apparently, I have to bunk with you tonight because she doesn't want me coming in late," he tells him.

"My couch has your name all over it," Walker offers.

"You should talk to Mom and Dad about renting Dallas's old place. It's just sitting there, vacant, since she and Beau moved into Myer's cabin," Payne tells him.

"Really? That'd be awesome. It's so close to Stoney Ridge," Foster agrees.

"Yes! That means, you can drive me around more often," Bellamy adds before reaching over and grabbing one of Walker's shots.

"Hey, that was mine, woman," Walker complains.

"Oh, sorry. I meant to grab this one," she says as she snatches another one and downs it.

"Dammit, we are going to have to deal with sloppy females tonight, fellas," Walker says as he shakes his head at her, but it's obvious he doesn't mind the least bit.

The band finally gets set up, and we order food as they begin their first set. They are good. A Southern rock sound, melding country and old classic rock 'n' roll, and they are a crowd-pleaser.

Bellamy and I switch seats, so she and the girls can chat over the music, and I overhear her filling them in on her disappointment with the Denver job being taken by that asshat she used to date. They are adequately outraged and keep ordering rounds of drinks to medicate their friend's pain.

"I didn't like him. There was just something about him," Sonia confesses.

"Liar! You told me you liked him a lot," Bellamy accuses.

"I didn't want to hurt your feelings and ruin your celebratory weekend. But you were obviously way too good for him. He was a tad skinny, and his ears were freakishly small," Sonia declares.

"She's right. You are definitely too hot for him," Elle agrees.

Bellamy turns to me. "They have to say that because they are my best friends."

I lean in and whisper-shout into her ear, "I have no doubt that it's the absolute truth."

Her eyes hit mine, and she smiles.

The first few chords of "Sweet Home Alabama" drift through the air, and Walker and Payne look at each other.

"Uh-oh, here we go," Payne says just as an inebriated Sonia throws her hands in the air.

"I love this song! You want to dance?" she asks a startled Foster.

He downs the rest of his beer and sets the bottle on the table. "Um, yes, I'd love to," he says.

He takes her hand, and she leads him out to the floor.

"What about you, Doc? Feel like cutting a rug with me?" Bellamy asks.

"I'm not much of a dancer," I tell her as she grabs my arm.

"Then, let me lead," she suggests.

"I can do that," I relent and follow her out on the dance floor.

"You're such a liar. You're a great dancer," she exclaims as I spin her around in a country two-step, tearing up the floor.

"I guess I can make do," I admit as I pull her in close.

"You are full of surprises, Dr. Haralson. If you aren't careful, I'm going to unlock all your mysteries," she warns.

"I just might let you," I whisper into her ear.

She grins at me before Elle grabs my hand and pulls us over toward her and Walker as another song begins. We laugh and dance until we are all covered in sweat, and the band takes a break.

Bellamy and her friends are so carefree, and being with them makes me feel the same.

If only it were that simple.

Sonia and Elle head to the ladies' room, and the rest of us go back to the table to order another round.

"I don't know what those first two things you did wrong today were exactly, but I know what that third one is," Walker goads Foster as we take our seats.

"It was just two friends dancing, man," Foster defends as his eyes follow Sonia and Elle.

"Maybe, but I've seen the way you watch her."

"So, she's beautiful. I know she's married and unavailable. Doesn't mean I'm not allowed to appreciate the beauty," he grumbles.

"She is, and of course you are," Bellamy tells him.

"Too bad you weren't single when she was," Walker adds.

"Yeah, too bad," Foster mumbles more to himself than to us.

When they return from the restroom, Sonia glances Foster's way, and a blush runs up her neck. I have a feeling the discussion in the ladies' room was much the same as the one here at the table.

"If you guys get loud, we might be able to convince Walker Reid to play a few with us. Whatcha think, Poplar Falls?" The lead singer makes the announcement from the stage, and a loud cheer rises from the crowd.

Walker jogs over, and one of the guys hands him a guitar. He swings it over his shoulder before the singer looks back at him.

"Get your ass up here, man. We want to hear that angelic voice of yours on this next one."

The band cues up Guns N' Roses' "Sweet Child O' Mine," and when Walker's voice hits the crowd, it sends a shock wave through the room.

"Damn, that boy is good," Payne praises.

"He sure is," Elle swoons.

Bellamy sighs as she lays her head on my shoulder and closes her eyes.

I like the feel of her curled into me. I like the feel of enjoying a night out with friends.

Content. That's what this is.

Seventeen

BRANDT

WE CLOSE DOWN THE BAR, PAY OUR TABS, AND WRANGLE the girls out to the parking lot. They are swaying and clinging to each other as they sing off-key. Walker tries to gently untangle their limbs, but Elle pulls them in tighter.

"I love you guys. Don't you worry about that SOB from Ohio, Bells. We'll find you a real man," she declares.

"Yeah," Sonia agrees as she stumbles, and Foster reaches out to keep her from falling on her ass. "Oops." She giggles.

A black sedan pulls in, and she straightens herself.

"That's my ride," she slurs as she breaks off and makes her way toward the vehicle, listing sideways.

"Are you kidding me?" Walker mumbles as he catches up to her and guides her to the passenger door. He opens it and helps her inside. He buckles her in as she waves and blows kisses back to the girls.

Once she is in and the door closes behind her, the car peels off in a cloud of dust.

Walker throws his hand in the air. "You're welcome for helping your wife into the car, douche bag," he calls after the taillights.

Elle and Bellamy are still holding on to each other with Foster keeping them steady.

"Come on, baby. Let's get you home." Walker beckons to Elle.

"I guess that means you're on my couch tonight, honey," Payne says as he slaps Foster's back.

"I expect breakfast in the morning, dear," Foster quips.

"Of course. I'm a gentleman."

"I have to drop Bellamy off, and I'll be right behind you," he tells Payne.

"I'll take her," I offer.

She looks up at me.

"I mean, it's on the way to town. That way, you don't have to backtrack," I clarify.

"It's okay by me if it's okay with you, Bells." Foster puts the ball in her court.

"Works for me," she says before taking off for my SUV.

"Glad you came out tonight, Doc," Payne says before offering me his hand.

I shake it and then Foster's.

"Yeah, you should come out with us more often," Foster agrees.

"I'll do that," I tell them.

Walker shouts his good-bye from his truck, and I join Bellamy in mine.

She's kicked her boots to the floorboard, and her feet are on the dash while she is focused on the radio. She has one eye closed and her tongue out in concentration as she turns all the knobs.

"It works better once I start the engine," I tease her, and she looks up.

"That's what the problem is," she says in exasperation.

"Yep," I say as I turn the key, and the music starts blaring at us.

She giggles as I turn the volume to an enjoyable level.

"You're an adorable drunk," I tell her.

"You're an adorable sober, Doc," she says on a hiccup. "I have a great idea. Let's get doughnuts," she blurts out.

"Doughnuts? It's two in the morning. I don't think there are any doughnut shops open around here at this hour," I tell her, and her face falls.

I lean in and whisper, "Tell you what."

She focuses her eyes on me and leans in too.

"I promise to have some doughnuts for you at the office in the morning."

"Thank you," she coos before her eyes widen. "Oh my goodness! I have to work in the morning. And my boss knows I've been out late, drinking!"

"I think he'll give you a pass this time."

"Whew, thank goodness. If I was still on ranch duty, Pop would probably make me sling manure till I puked."

That makes me bark out a laugh.

"Let's get you home, so you can sleep it off before it's time to clock in."

"Okay," she says before a yawn escapes, and she closes her eyes.

By the time we make it to Stoney Ridge, she is fast asleep.

I slowly pull up the drive and leave the engine running as I round the front of the truck and open her door. I try to wake her, but she mumbles something incoherent and pulls her legs into a ball under her.

I wrap an arm under her and gently lift her, and she sighs and leans into me. I move her to get a better grip around her waist and feed my other arm under her legs, lifting her from the seat. The front porch light blinks on, and Winston Wilson steps out. He stands and waits as I carefully make my way to him while holding a sleeping Bellamy close to my chest.

"I'm sorry we woke you," I apologize as I climb the steps.

"You didn't. It's the darnedest thing. I know she's grown, but if we expect her home, I can't fall off until I know she's tucked safely in her bed," he says as we make it to him, and he opens his arms to take her weight from me.

She stirs as I transfer her to her father's embrace.

"Poppy," she mutters, "I want doughnuts."

He laughs quietly as her eyes drift back closed, and her breath evens out.

"She would randomly ask for doughnuts when she was little. At night before bed, during her riding lessons, at church while the reverend was in the middle of his sermon. Silly baby. She'll always be my little girl—whether she's twenty-five, thirty-five, or even when she's sixty-five. I'll worry, and I'll carry her for as long as I'm able. Or until the Lord sends someone else to do the job for me," he says as he looks adoringly at her, curled in his arms.

A parent's love is powerful.

"I hate that we kept you up," I tell him.

"I don't mind at all, son. I'm glad she had a good night. Her mother tells me it's been a rough week for her."

"Yeah," I agree.

"Thank you for making sure she got home safe."

"My pleasure," I reply as I smile down at her.

She looks like an angel in her daddy's arms.

He clears his throat.

"Oh, um, I'll get her boots. I'll be right back."

I turn and hurry to the Rover. I pluck her discarded boots from the floorboard and take them back. Winston has already carried Bellamy in and made his way back to the door. I hand him her shoes.

"Good night, Doc. We'll see you tomorrow." He bids me farewell, and I make my way home.

It was a fun night. I can't remember the last time I actually went out and enjoyed myself so much.

When I make it to my apartment, Lou-Lou greets me at the door. I walk her, and then I take a quick shower before settling in.

I fall right off to sleep and have a dreamless reprieve until the alarm starts blaring at eight a.m.

Five uninterrupted hours of rest. I can't remember the last time that happened either.

I rush over to Bountiful Harvest and pick up an assortment of dough-nuts before Bellamy arrives at the office.

Her face lights up when she enters the break room to start the cof-fee and finds them sitting beside a full pot.

Seeing her delight as she takes a bite of the powdered-sugar con-fection makes the rush this morning completely worth it.

She is radiant in her pantsuit and heels. You'd never guess she was three sheets to the wind only a few hours ago.

"We have a light schedule today, Doc," she says around a bite.

I reach out and wipe sugar from the corner of her mouth. Her eyes soften at my touch, and I quickly pull my hand back before I ab-sentmindedly lick the sugar from my thumb. Then, her eyes widen.

I clear my throat. "I, um, I scheduled us light today on purpose. It's Friday, and the new granite is being delivered to the house tomor-row, so I want to get over there and knock out all of the old cabinets and counters," I begin to babble.

She claps and does a little hop on her heels. "Oh, does that mean I get to help?" she asks hopefully.

I look down the length of her. "You aren't exactly dressed for dem-olition," I observe.

"I'll call Momma and ask her to drop some jeans by for me. Please?" she begs.

"Sure. Four hands are better than two" I give in.

"Yes!"

The bell over the door chimes, signaling the beginning of our day.

"Thank you for the doughnuts, Doc," she says as she scoots past me and sashays out to greet our first client.

"You are very welcome, Miss Wilson," I mumble to myself.

Eighteen

BELLAMY

WE WORK STEADILY ALL MORNING, SEEING PATIENTS, AND I assist Brandt in several procedures. He is thorough and teaches me proper techniques as we vaccinate, stitch, swab, X-ray, and cast the pups, kitties, and even an ornery rooster that came through the door. He is so good with not only the animals, but also with their owners. Kind, informative, comforting, and patient with all their concerns and questions.

During a short break between clients, I step out to take a walk and decide to finally accept Derrick's call when his name pops up on my phone screen.

"Bellamy," he breathes in relief.

"Hey, Derrick."

It's all I say, and the silence lingers between us as he works up the courage to say his piece.

"I'm sorry," he starts.

"You should be," I interrupt.

"I hope that you've had a few days to think things over and you're able to see that this is a good thing for us."

Did he just say that?

"Really, Derrick? You know, I thought that maybe *you* had a few days to think things over and were calling to be contrite and offer me a real apology or maybe retract your acceptance of the job."

"Why would I do that? It's the perfect opportunity for me to land in the same city you are so hell-bent on living in. I thought this was something we would celebrate. Once I'm in, I can find you a spot with ease. We both win," he says, and I catch the irritation in his voice.

"You cannot honestly tell me you thought I'd be celebrating you stealing the position I wanted. That I'd worked so hard to get. No one is that oblivious," I accuse.

"Give me six months. I'll apply for the director position when Singh retires, and I'll give you the damn job," he bites out.

The arrogance. *Has he always been this cocky, or was I the oblivious one?*

"You know what? You do whatever you want. I don't care, but I'll get my own job, thank you, and my own apartment, and I'll live my own life. Enjoy yours!"

I hit the End Call button. Then, I immediately go to my Contacts list and scroll down to block his number.

When I make it back to the office, I stomp in past Brandt and sit behind the desk. I start typing the notes from the last patient into the computer.

He watches me closely and then speaks, "Our one o'clock called and canceled. You want to get closed up and get out of here?"

I hit Save and look up. I meet his eyes before clicking the computer screen off in the affirmative. "Let's go."

I pull the safety goggles over my eyes. I attempt to raise the sledge-hammer over my head to rain my pent-up fury down on the cabinets hanging above the sink when a firm hand grabs the handle and tugs it from my grip.

"Hey, I was about to bust some shit up," I exclaim as relief crawls up the back of my arms when the weight of the massive tool falls from my grasp.

"Yeah, you were about to bust open your own head with this thing," he says, trying to stifle a laugh.

I cock a hip, place my hand on it, and glare at him. "I'll have you know that I'm stronger than I look. I was raised on a ranch, and I can sling hay bales with the best of them," I inform him with more than a hint of attitude.

"I have no doubt," he responds, "but how about you use this one and let me handle the beast?"

I stare at the small hammer he has extended toward me and scowl.

"It'll still do some damage, trust me. Please, for the sake of my ego," he urges as he shakes the pitiful gadget at me.

I give in on a sigh. "Oh, all right. I wouldn't want your manhood to take a hit."

I snatch the hammer from his grip and turn to start pounding at the tacky laminate countertop. The snap and pop of the flimsy surface satisfies my need to destroy something. Or more like *someone*. I picture Derrick's placating face as I rip through the wood like butter.

I'm startled when a boom from across the room sends slivers of splintered wood flying past me. Brandt has the sledgehammer hoisted above him and slams it into a cabinet, knocking it from its mounting in one fell swoop.

I guess he has a few demons to exorcise himself.

We continue to work in silent companionship for the next hour or so until we have completely demolished the entire kitchen. When the final shards of material hit the floor, I look over to see a sweaty Brandt breathing heavily as he drops his weapon at his feet with a loud thud. His soaking-wet white T-shirt is practically transparent and clinging to every chiseled muscle as he gulps in air.

Damn, that's sexy.

I thought he was attractive before, but I never realized how truly beautiful he was.

He stares at the mess scattered at our feet for a few moments, lost in another place, and then he runs his hands through his hair as he blinks a few times. His eyes meet mine, like he just realized I was still here or that he was.

"I bet your arms are like Jell-O, aren't they?" I ask.

He takes a moment to assess himself. He rolls his shoulders and squeezes his hands open and closed a few times before answering me on a grin, "Yeah, I'll be paying for this tomorrow for sure."

His eyes cut behind me, and he surveys the condition of the L-shaped countertop—or what's left of it.

"Looks like you got a workout too," he surmises from the pile of wreckage.

"It deserved its fate for being such an offensive shade of avocado," I tell him without looking from his flushed face.

He chuckles. "That it did," he agrees.

I watch in fascination as he tugs up the end of his shirt to bring it up and wipe the rivulet of sweat running down his forehead. I'm treated to a glimpse of a light smattering of dark curls that leads the way down his chest to a golden six-pack, which veers down below the band of his jeans.

Oh my.

As my eyes crawl back up his body, I see the dimple pop from the grin as he catches me ogling him.

I clear my throat and turn quickly to hide the blush that I'm sure is spreading up my neck.

"What's next, Doc?" I ask to my feet as I sweep plaster and dust into a heap with the toe of my boot.

"Are you hungry?" he asks.

I look up at him. "Um, not really, no," I say hesitantly.

His eyes travel around the room. "We're not going to find anything to eat in here anyway. How about a drink?" he asks.

Drinks?

He must see the question flash across my face because he quickly adds, "I have a bottle of tequila or whiskey, whichever you prefer. I think we've both worked up a thirst." Then, he says softly, "The least I can do is help you quench it."

He leans in and reaches around me to open the freezer of the old fridge still standing to the side of the mess we created to show me the bottles.

"You mean, I'm not getting paid for this? You should have told me that, and I would have clocked out today. Sucks to be you, I guess," I tease as I turn on my heels and strut to the hall bathroom. "I'll be right back, and I'll have the tequila," I toss over my shoulder.

I hear his quiet laughter as I lock the door. I let out the breath I was holding and chastise myself in the mirror.

He is your boss, Bellamy Wilson, and he is unavailable. He made that very clear. So, get your libido under control and stop thinking about his pecs and abs this instant!

"Temporary boss," I tell my reflection.

"Did you say something?" His question comes muffled from the other side of the door.

Shit.

"Nope," I squeak. "Just humming to myself."

I wait silently as my lie lingers between us.

"Okay. Meet you on the porch in ten," he says before I hear his heavy footfalls heading up the stairs to the master suite.

I sag against the back of the door in relief.

Nineteen

BRANDT

BELLAMY TAKES A LONG TIME IN THE BATHROOM. I USED THE facilities upstairs and came back down to grab the tequila from the freezer. I have been out here on the porch for at least fifteen minutes before the door finally opens and she emerges.

"Hey," she says as she presses her back against the closed door and watches me.

"Hey yourself. I was about to send a search party in for you," I tease.

"I tried to splash water on all my sweaty parts, and then there wasn't a towel, so I had to air-dry the best I could," she explains.

"I thought you smelled a little better," I rib her.

She looks up at that comment. "Oh, really? You don't exactly smell like a bouquet of roses yourself there, Doc," she playfully snaps back before coming forward and taking the tequila bottle from my hand.

"I didn't think to pick up any mixers—or any glasses for that matter," I tell her as she walks over and sits down on the railing.

She pops open the top of the bottle. "I guess we'll just have to make do, then," she says before throwing her head back and taking a huge swig.

I watch as the muscles in her slender neck ripple as she swallows. Then, she squeezes her eyes shut as the alcohol burns its way down. She opens them and looks at me as she wipes her lips with the back of her hand. Then, she extends the bottle out in invitation.

"This is probably a bad idea on empty stomachs," I say as I walk over and take it from her fingers.

"Come on, Doc. Live dangerously," she dares with a twinkle in her eye.

I decide to do just that, and I take a long pull from the bottle. My eyes never leave hers as I pass it back to her.

She glances over her shoulder and muses, "Looks like the sun is setting behind the mountains."

I follow her gaze and take in her silhouette, bathed in the blaze of pinks and oranges, peppered with purple from the colors streaked across the sky behind her.

"Breathtaking," I murmur.

She silently stares off into the distance as she continues to sip from the clear bottle.

Once the sun finally disappears, she breathes in a deep breath. She hops down from the railing and takes a seat on the concrete steps that lead up to the porch. Then, she looks back at me and pats the spot beside her.

I sit next to her, and she hands me the bottle. I take another gulp.

She lays her chin on my shoulder, and I peer down at her. Her eyes are glazed over, and she is studying me. I take another shot from the bottle and notice the liquor slides down my throat easily this time. Instead of burning, it warms my body.

Bellamy moves her hand to reach for the bottle and take her turn just as I raise it to offer. Her hand drops to my lap instead, and rather than pull it away, her eyes follow it down and she holds it in place. My cock twitches at her near brush, and her hand is a hairbreadth from feeling its reaction.

I hear her quick intake of breath, so I know she's noticed.

I try to reposition myself to hide my body's involuntary response when she lightly grazes my growing arousal with the back of her hand. I slightly buck up off the step at the contact.

"Bells," I huff out hoarsely, and her eyes come to mine. Her big, beautiful stormy-blue eyes.

She opens her mouth to say something, but she doesn't get the chance because, without thinking, I bring my hand to her chin and rub my thumb over her bottom lip. I bend my head and slightly brush my mouth against hers. Her eyes widen in surprise, but she doesn't move.

I pull back as I drop my hand from her face and start to apologize, "I'm so—"

I don't get the words out before she bears up and grasps my neck, pulling me back to her mouth.

All thought of an apology flies from my mind as she opens to the kiss, and her tongue darts tentatively against my lips. I part for her and then deepen our connection as I wrap my arms around her back and bring her body closer to mine.

She slides a leg over my hips and seats herself astride me without breaking our contact. It's been so long since I was in such intimate proximity with a woman. My body takes over, and my hands slide down to the back pockets of her jeans. I clasp her ass and move her against me as she winds her arms around my shoulders and laces her fingers into my hair.

All the despair and loneliness of the last few years melt away, and all that matters at this moment is the feel of the woman in my arms and the glide of our tongues wrestling as we fight to get as close as possible to each other.

I break from the kiss and drop my forehead to hers. The intoxicating smell of tequila surrounds us as our breaths intermingle. I glide my hand up and move it across the pulse throbbing at her throat. Then, I bring my lips to the spot and lay a soft kiss there. She closes her eyes, and her head falls back to give me better access to her neck. I slide my tongue down to her collarbone, tasting the sweet saltiness of her glistening skin. She moans slightly as I suck at the hollow spot just where her throat meets the top of her chest, and her breathing grows ragged.

She releases my hair and runs her hands down my back and around to my sides. Gripping the hem of my tee, she pulls it up, and her hands roam my chest. Her fingers tug slightly at the hair she finds there before her nails score lightly down my abs. My mouth moves from the base of her throat, lower, lavishing attention just above her breast. My cock grows painfully hard between us, and I raise my hips from the step to nestle it into her heat.

She gasps and presses down heavy on me.

I groan.

She wiggles her hips a little, and I dig my fingers into her ass as I try to keep myself from rocketing off the steps and laying her out on the damn dirty porch.

She buries her face into my neck and whispers, "Brandt."

"Yes, baby?" I manage to respond.

"I need to talk to Elle," is her peculiar reply.

"Right now?" I ask.

She nods into my neck, and I move my hand up to the space between her shoulder blades and hold her to me.

"Okay, I can take you to Elle," I tell her.

She lifts her head and brings her face close to mine. Our lips almost touching, she says, "Girl code."

"Girl code?" I ask.

"Girl code," she repeats.

Then, she presses another sweet, long kiss to my mouth before she starts to shift, and I groan again as I help her stand.

She extends her hand to me, and I take it as I come off the step.

"Are you okay to drive?" she asks.

"Yep, completely sober now," I say as I adjust myself, and she giggles.

I gather the bottle as she goes inside and starts to turn off all the lights.

We lock up, and then I drive her to Rustic Peak. She texts as I drive, and when we pull into the gate, Elle and Walker are sitting on the swing, waiting for us to arrive.

Walker stands and kisses Elle's cheek before descending the steps and opening the door for Bellamy.

She looks back at me as she scoots out. "I had a really good day with you, Doc."

"I had a good day with you too."

She smiles and then slides out. She walks to join Elle on the swing.

Walker is still standing with the passenger door open, and he looks in at me.

"Wanna go for a beer?" he asks.

"Sure."

I don't even get the word out before he swings up into the seat and shuts the door.

"I know the perfect spot," he says, and I throw the truck in gear.

Twenty

BELLAMY

"**W**ELL?" ELLE ASKS AS WE SIT AND SWING.

"Um, I …" I start and then stop again. Trying to figure out how to explain what happened between Brandt and me.

I turn to face her and just blurt it all out, "I finally talked to Derrick this afternoon. I thought maybe he was sorry and we could talk like adults, but the jackass just kept trying to justify himself. While he was talking, I realized that I didn't even like him very much. He's handsome in a buttoned-up kind of way, but I think I was just lonely in Chicago. He was nice, but I didn't quiver when we kissed. Does that make sense? Anyway, I told him exactly what I thought of him before hanging up on him and blocking his number. I was so pissed at that point that I took a hammer to Brandt's house."

"A hammer?" she interrupts.

"Yeah." I roll my eyes as I continue, "I wanted the sledgehammer, but Brandt didn't think I could lift it, and he was probably right. I had one, maybe two, good swings of it in me, and then I would have been done for sure. So, I took the pitiful little hammer he gave me, and I did some damage with it, let me tell you."

She looks perplexed as she tries her best to follow my rambling.

"After we wore ourselves out, annihilating the gosh-awful kitchen, we decided to get wasted on tequila. We didn't have any mixers or glasses, so we basically just chugged it straight up from the bottle, which wasn't the brightest idea either of us had ever had. I guess, with the alcohol and all that pent-up aggression being released, we were on some sort of euphoric high, you know what I mean?"

She shakes her head like she has no clue, but I power through anyway.

"The sunset was so pretty, and he looked so good, all sweaty and disheveled. Have you ever seen him without a shirt on? Who knew he was hiding all that muscle and that V that looks so good on a man, you know? I think the tequila went to my head, and one thing led to another and … and …"

"And?" she prompts impatiently.

"And I might have made a move on him." I cover my face with my hands as I fill with embarrassment, bracing for her scolding.

"Then, what?" she asks, exasperated.

I peek at her through my fingers.

"Then, we made out for a while," I mumble into my hands.

"You made out with Brandt," she says as she grabs the tips of my fingers and pulls my hands down.

"Yes. Are you mad?"

"Mad? Why would I be mad?" she asks, and her question sounds confused.

"Because I made out with a man you used to date."

She raises her left hand and points to the diamond sitting on her finger, giving me a look that says, *Duh.*

"I know, but it's still not polite to come on to your best friend's ex," I remind her.

"I don't consider Brandt an ex. He and I had dinner a few times, and we never made it past a quick kiss. Not even a real *kiss*, kiss," she insists.

"So, you don't care that I threw myself at him?"

She laughs. "Not at all, but I want details."

I frown at her.

"What? I said I didn't care."

"Yeah, well, now, I'm just kind of regretting stopping in the middle and insisting he bring me here," I mutter.

"In the middle?" Her eyes get round as saucers.

I open my mouth to clarify, and she brings her hand up.

"Stop. Sonia will kill us if you go any further in this story without her here. Let's go in. I'll text her and tell her to get over here ASAP, and we'll make cookies while we wait."

She stands, and I follow her inside. When we make it to the kitchen, Doreen is at the sink, washing her hands.

"Bellamy, I didn't know you were coming by," Doreen greets as I take a seat at the table.

"She didn't either. She had to come to tell me she made out with Brandt this evening. I'm going to get Sonia over here, so Bells can give us details. We will need cookies," Elle explains as she picks up the phone on the wall and dials.

Doreen looks at me. "Chocolate chip or oatmeal raisin?"

It takes Sonia exactly twelve minutes to make the twenty-minute drive from her house to Rustic Peak.

In that time, Doreen has whipped together cookie dough and is adding the balls to a greased pan.

I go back over everything I told Elle on the swing. A little calmer this go-around. Doreen and Sonia listen intently.

"And now, here we are," I finish as the timer on the oven goes off, startling us.

Sonia sits back in her chair and blows out a long breath. "Well, that's a lot of information to process. Let's start with Derrick," she begins.

"Derrick!" Elle protests.

Sonia gives her a stern glare. "Yes, Derrick. Now, I'm happy you shook him off. You deserve better than a weasel who goes behind your back and doesn't discuss what he's doing. How do you feel about cutting him loose? Any residual regret? Second thoughts?" she prods.

"No. I feel relieved, to be honest. I didn't realize how stressed out I had been about trying to make the relationship work with us in different states until it wasn't an issue any longer."

"Okay, onto busting shit up. Did you really destroy Brandt and his mother's kitchen? That seems extreme, even for you."

"Even for me? What does that mean?"

"I mean, you are impulsive and a bit crazy sometimes, but you know that, so move on and answer the question," Sonia demands.

"It's his new house. He bought the Sugarman Homestead, and he's remodeling. We tore the kitchen out because he's having it completely redone."

"He bought our house?" she gasps. Then, she looks at Elle and asks, "Did you know that?"

Elle nods. "He told me at lunch the other day. Cool, right?"

"Yes, cool!" She turns back to me. "He's going to live in that big, old house all by himself?"

"Him and his mom. But you know, it's not nearly as massive as we thought it was. I mean, it looked humongous to our little-girl eyes, but it's just a tad bigger than this place, to tell you the truth. We never could have raised three families in there."

"Really?" She sounds disappointed.

"It's still a good size, and it's gorgeous—or it will be when he finishes," I reassure her.

"I bet. I can't wait to see that place finally fixed up," she says.

"Same," Elle interjects.

"Now, onto the next part. Tequila and kissing. How did all that start?"

I look over at Doreen, who is using a spatula to transfer cookies from the pan to a plate.

She looks over her shoulder at us. "Don't stop on my account. I want to know too," she insists.

"Um, I don't think I can talk about this in front of you," I tell her.

"Oh, for goodness' sake, why not? I'm a woman too. I know what it feels like to be excited by a man."

"Aunt Doe," Elle howls.

"Well, I do."

"Fine," I say, and then I proceed to recount every detail from the time I reached for the tequila and missed to me asking Brandt to bring me here to see Elle.

"Wow," Sonia declares.

"Yes, wow," Doreen and Elle agree.

"So, where did you leave things?" Sonia asks.

"Just like that," I say.

"You didn't tell him why you'd stopped and insisted on talking to Elle?" Sonia asks.

"Well, kind of. I told him it was girl code."

"Girl code? He has no idea what girl code is. He probably thinks you're a tease. Or insane," she yells.

"I'm sure he could deduce what she meant by girl code," Doreen adds.

"You think?" I ask.

She reaches across the table and reassuringly covers my hand with hers. "If not, I'm sure Walker is filling him in right about now."

Perfect.

Twenty-One

BRANDT

WALKER HAS ME DRIVE OVER TO BRAXTON AND SOPHIE'S house. Braxton is sitting on the deck with his feet propped up on a cooler when we arrive.

I park and follow Walker as he ascends the steps up to the puppy gate and lets us through it.

"So, the women ran you two off, huh?" Braxton says as we take a seat in the other two Adirondack chairs that face out to the gorge.

"Yep, best-friend crisis," Walker says as Braxton reaches into the cooler and tosses him and then me a beer.

"What was it this time?" he asks.

Walker shrugs. "Don't know, but if I were a betting man, I'd say, Doc here knows."

Both their eyes come to me, and they wait.

"All Bellamy said was girl code," I offer them the only information I have.

Walker's eyes widen.

"What does that mean?" I ask.

"Why, it means that Miss Wilson has caught interest in you, Doc," he declares.

I wrinkle my brow. "Caught interest in me?"

"Yep. See, in women's language, girl code means that one of them likes a dude the other of them has either liked, crushed on, or dated in the past. The girl then has to get the all clear from the other one that it's okay to proceed with said love interest. If girl number one doesn't give girl number two the permission to pursue said old flame, then it's game over. They never bring it up again. First girl's claim trumps the new girl's affection even if it was never reciprocated by said old flame," he explains.

"Can a guy be considered an old flame if he was never a flame to begin with?" I ask for clarification.

"In chick world, abso-fuckin'-lutely."

"Really?"

"Yep. It doesn't make sense, but then again, it doesn't have to make sense to us. It does to them," Braxton confirms.

"So, Bellamy wanted to talk to Elle about me?"

"Correct, sir. You did go out with my girl a time or two last year," Walker points out.

"But Elle and I are just friends. We've only ever been friends," I assure him.

"Doesn't matter. You guys went out, so Bells is going to make sure Elle is okay with her tickling your pickle," he insists.

"You and Elle are engaged," I state.

"Yep."

"That doesn't make any sense."

"Like Brax said, it doesn't have to. They are chicks."

Braxton nods his agreement.

"Tickle my pickle?"

"If you're lucky," Walker says and grins at me before he takes another pull from his beer.

"That's not going to happen. I think Bellamy is a sweet girl, but—"

Walker cuts me off, "Sweet girl? She's gorgeous. And she's into you. I could tell the other night at the bar. So, why won't it happen? Are you carrying a torch for my woman, Doc?"

"No."

"Then, what's the problem? If it's Myer, don't worry. He might sucker punch you when he finds out, but he'll eventually come around."

Braxton cuts his eyes to Walker. "That's still debatable."

"You love me, and you know it." Walker blows off his comment.

"I'm just not someone she wants to get involved with."

"Why not? You're a good-looking dude. Successful. Good to your momma. What's wrong with you? You got a secret girlfriend or a lovechild back in Oregon or something?" Walker digs.

"No, not a girlfriend. A wife."

All humor falls from Walker's face, and both he and Braxton focus their big-brother stares on me.

"Come again?" Braxton bites.

"Her name is Annie. *Was*. Her name was Annie. She was killed by a stranger in a restaurant parking lot almost three years ago."

Walker whistles low, and they both sit back heavy in their chairs.

"Damn, man. I'm sorry to hear that." All humor is gone from Walker's voice as he takes on a serious tone for the first time ever in my presence.

This is why I don't share. I hate the pity that people instantly feel when they hear the words.

"What happened exactly?" Braxton is focused on me, but he isn't offering sympathy or feigning pain over a woman he has never met.

"It was our wedding anniversary. We had reservations at her favorite Italian restaurant in town. I promised I wouldn't be late. My practice was new, and I was always working. Always running late or missing everything important to her. I insisted I'd be there. Then, I got held up at the office.

"A lady came in, and she was in a panic about her dog, just as I was trying to lock up. The dog was having a seizure. The poor woman was a mess. So, I brought them in and looked the dog over. It was an older dog. I texted Annie to tell her I would be there as soon as I could, and I waited with the lady until the seizure passed and she was calm. Then, I sent them to the emergency clinic.

"Angry, Annie had texted back not to bother, to go ahead and treat the dog. I hurried to the place as fast as I could, hoping to catch her before she was gone. I made it just in time to watch a vagrant slit her throat with a dirty blade and yank her purse she was clinging to. She bled out in my arms before police or medics could make it to the scene."

Until now, I haven't told that story out loud to anyone since the trial. Not a single soul.

"Did they catch him?" Braxton asks.

"Yeah. I was able to describe him and tell them the direction he had taken off in. They found him in an abandoned house with a needle in his arm a few hours later. He used the twenty-three dollars Annie had had in her wallet to buy a single hit of heroin. He'd killed my wife for a thirty-minute high."

"Fuck," Walker utters.

"It's good they got him," Braxton affirms.

"Yeah. But he wasn't the only one responsible. I should be rotting in that cell right beside him," I mutter more to myself than to them.

"Are you shittin' me?" Walker asks.

Braxton puts his hand up, and Walker halts what he was about to say.

"You been carrying that shit on you all this time?" Braxton asks the baffling question.

"Shit?"

"Yeah, that guilt you have sitting on your chest like an anchor."

I don't respond as he bores his eyes into mine. It's like he can see all the way to my soul.

Then, he starts his story. "It was early November. We were on our way to cut down a Christmas tree at Kringle's Tree Farm. We usually waited until after Thanksgiving to get one, but it had snowed that weekend, and since Aunt Madeline and her new beau were coming for a visit, Momma wanted to go ahead and decorate the house and start being festive a little early that year. It was the first time we were getting to meet Jefferson Lancaster, and she wanted everything to be perfect for Aunt Mads.

"I remember Dad and I were outside, shoveling the drive and walkway, when she came out of the house with Elle on her hip, all bundled up, and they ambushed us with snowballs. We spent that afternoon together, laughing and playing in the snow. Then, I helped her convince Dad to load us all up into his Cherokee to go get a tree. It took us both. He wanted to wait because he said the tree would be too dried out by Christmas, but I begged him. Elle was so excited. It was the first Christmas she was old enough to grasp the idea of Santa and presents. He finally gave in after I promised to keep it well watered every day.

"I can still see that entire ride vividly. Momma popped in a CD and made us all sing carols. Elle was clapping, and Dad was purposefully getting all the words wrong while I laughed. The car came out of nowhere. The last thing I remember before we were hit was my mother's face looking back at us and going from a wide, happy smile to pure panic. I didn't have time to turn and see what she saw before I heard the sound of wheels squealing and steel crunching. She was in a seat belt, but she managed to snake her arms out and twist in the seat like lightning, trying to reach us and shield us with her body. The impact was so hard it slung us around in circles and threw her against the windshield. Her head slammed into the glass and busted open. We went over the side and I remember the feel of falling, and when we slammed into the ground, part of the frame broke loose and ended up imbedded in her chest. Her body was shaking from the shock. I tried so hard to get loose and get to her, but I was trapped. I swear, for years, every time I closed my eyes, I could hear her petrified screams."

I watch him get lost in that memory as he closes his eyes tightly, and the pain washes over him.

"I've never told anyone that. Not even Elle," he confesses.

"I'm so sorry," I tell him.

"We ended up upside down at the bottom of the gap. It took rescuers forever to reach us. Momma went silent fairly quickly, and I could hear Dad's anguished cries as he reached for her face. He was coughing blood. I remember the gurgling sound when he tried to talk. Elle was screaming as she hung from her car seat. He struggled to get free, but he was pinned, and his chest was crushed by the steering wheel. I was dazed, but I was able to finally get my belt undone, and through my sobs, I asked him what to do. He told me to take care of my sister. I crawled over and grabbed her, got her loose, and wrapped her in my arms. We sat there, huddled on the roof of the SUV, with him reassuring us that everything would be okay as he lost his fight. He took his last breath as the sirens filled the air, and lights from the sheriff's car and ambulance reflected on the back windshield. He held on until that moment. Until he knew help had arrived for us. Then, he took one last labored breath. He hadn't wanted to leave us alone in that wreck."

"*Jeezus*," is all I can manage to say.

"I blamed myself, just like you, for a long time. I was the reason we had been out that night. I convinced him to go get the tree. If I hadn't promised to water it, he wouldn't have given in. It was all my fault," he says as he looks up at me.

I shake my head. He was just a kid. It was an accident.

"When I ended up here with Aunt Madeline and Jefferson, I was so closed off. I was afraid to get close to them. Afraid to love them. I thought I didn't deserve love. In the beginning, the only thing that kept me going was Elle. I had to take care of Elle."

He stops for a moment and gets a far-off look. One I know well.

"Hard to tell which is worse sometimes. Being the one dying or the one left behind."

I nod in agreement.

"Guess we won't know till we're dead," Walker utters.

"Survivor's guilt. That's what Gram called it," Braxton goes on. "See, I was angry and grieving. It took me a long time to realize that I hadn't killed them. The drunk driver plowing into us had killed them. It was an accident. It could have happened anytime. While they were on the way to the store, going to work, or at a gas station. It could have happened with or without us in the truck. It could have happened that night or four weeks from that night on our way to get a tree if we had decided to wait. Accidents are just that … accidents and they're senseless. And it was not my fault. Gram helped me see that.

"Brandt, what happened to your wife was not your fault. She was leaving the restaurant early because you were late. So? She could have been attacked on the way out while you paid the bill, or you could have walked out of that door together and been attacked. She'd still be the one who lost her life, and you still would have lived. It could have happened at any time or anywhere when she wasn't with you. You are not to blame because you were running late. The man with the knife and the evil intent is the one to blame."

He brings his eyes to meet mine, and I can see the truth in them.

"You didn't kill her, brother."

"I do every night when I relive that moment in my dreams," I tell him.

"Because you don't believe it yet, but hear me. You did not kill her."

"You did not kill her," Walker repeats.

Twenty-Two

BELLAMY

I END UP CALLING HOME AND TELLING MY PARENTS THAT I AM STAYING the night with Elle.

We continue to dissect the evening's events over two plates of cookies. Ria joins us for plate number two, and she lets us in on a conversation she had with Elaine while they had coffee one morning.

Apparently, Brandt is a widower.

"Well, that explains a lot," Elle says after Ria breaks the news.

She says she always felt something from his past was holding him back from opening up fully. Ria doesn't know the circumstances surrounding his wife's death but just that it was out of the blue and that Brandt did not cope very well with her loss.

"She hoped that moving here would help him heal," Ria says.

"I'm not sure he has," I share.

"No, not completely, not yet," she agrees.

We end the night somberly, all curled up in the living room, watching reruns of *Gilmore Girls*, like we did when we were younger, until the aunts fall asleep, and Sonia leaves to go home to Ricky.

I don't sleep much. I toss and turn all night, thinking of how painful it must be for Brandt and wondering if I made things worse for him.

By the time the sun comes up, I have decided to back off and pretend it was just the tequila and no big deal.

Hopefully, work won't be too awkward on Monday morning. Thank goodness we have the weekend.

We get up and help Ria and Doreen make breakfast before the ranch hands show up, hungry. Once everyone has eaten, Elle goes off to take a shower, and Sophie and I use the opportunity to sit Doreen down and discuss the fake engagement party.

Sophie put a deposit on Mystic Mill, which is an old sawmill outside of town that has been converted into a special-event venue. It is a gorgeous space that hosts everything from weddings to retirement parties to political fundraisers for the people of Poplar Falls.

Doreen gets excited at the news.

"I love that place," she remarks. "It's big and romantic. The perfect venue."

Sophie smiles and then asks our input on food.

"We can help with that. Ria and I will make the food," Doreen chirps.

"Um, I'm going to hire someone to do the food," Sophie insists.

"Why on earth would you do that? We know all her favorites, and we are more than happy to do it."

"Because, Aunt Doe, if you two are in this kitchen for days, cooking enough food to feed the town, Elle will catch on to it. Besides, I need you to be the one keeping her distracted and get her to the party."

"Me? Why me? I'm sure Bellamy and Sonia can get her there."

Sophie looks panicked for a moment, and I weigh in.

"It's the weekend of the church's mother-daughter dinner, and Elle and I bought tickets. She plans to ask you to go with her and Momma and me. Just act surprised when she asks you, okay?"

"She wants me to go to a mother-daughter dinner with her?" Doreen asks.

"That's what she said," I tell her, and it's not a lie. Elle does plan to take her. The dinner is just the weekend after.

"What about Madeline?" she asks.

I shrug. "She said she wanted you to come."

"Oh goodness," she says as she dabs at her eyes with a kitchen towel.

"Don't cry, or she's going to get suspicious. You're going to have to miss the dinner anyway," Ria reminds her.

"Oh no, you girls already spent the money," she cries.

"It's fine. It's for charity, and a big ole engagement party is way better," I assure her.

"Yep, it will be," Sophie agrees. "Now, let's discuss the food."

"You should call Flying Horse Catering in Aurora. They're excellent," Ria suggests.

"Oh, that's a splendid idea," Doreen agrees. "I love their food. It's so good, and the staff is amazing. They catered my friend Nancy's daughter's wedding. I highly recommend them."

Sophie grins. "Done. I'll call them today."

Elle comes walking in with her hair in a ponytail and her riding gear on.

The room goes silent.

"What?" she asks as she strolls to the fridge and grabs a pitcher of juice.

"Nothing, sweetie. We were just talking more about Bellamy and Brandt," Doreen covers.

"Bellamy and Brandt?!" Sophie says, and her eyes fly to me.

"Yes, Bellamy. And. Brandt," Doreen enunciates clearly while staring at Sophie.

Sophie nods. "Yeah, they were filling me in."

"Well, I hope you two explore things," Elle says without missing a beat.

"I thought about it last night, and I think, in light of his story, it's not such a good idea after all."

"Why not?" Elle asks.

"He's probably not ready, and I just broke up with Derrick twenty-four hours ago."

"His wife has been gone for a few years, and it's not like you and Derrick were that serious. There's nothing wrong with you both moving on," she insists.

"I guess we'll wait and see what happens," I decide.

"Good plan, dear," Ria agrees with me.

Twenty-Three

BRANDT

"I'M MUCH OBLIGED YOU CAME ALL THE WAY OUT HERE ON A Saturday, Dr. Haralson."

I follow the farmer out past his dairy barns to the pen holding the goats in question.

"Here they are. All three of them have had a dry cough for over a week. At first, I thought maybe it was just allergies, so I separated them from the rest of the herd to keep an eye on them, and we've been dumping their milk, just in case."

"All right, let's have a look."

I enter the pen and thoroughly examine the animals.

"Well?"

"Looks like you have a lungworm infection," I break the news to him.

He removes his hat and scratches his head. "That's what I figured."

"To be safe, we should treat the entire herd. If you get them rounded up, I'll dose them today, and that should kill any adult parasites. Then, we'll schedule a second dosing in two weeks to catch any of the larvae that might have hatched. I'll prescribe a probiotic to balance out their digestive tract, and you'll just add it to their feed for the next three days. We'll also supplement with iron to quickly rebuild their blood cell count. You'll have to dump a couple more times, and then they should be good as new. But we'll give them the anti-parasitic again in six months because it can live that long out in your pasture."

"I only got one hand today, and he's running the milking parlor. My other one is down with the flu. It'll take me a bit to round the herd."

"Not a problem. I'll run to my office to get the medication, and I'll call and see if my assistant is available to help with the dosing."

He nods and walks off toward the barn. I take my phone out and dial Bellamy's number.

"Hello?" she asks tentatively.

"Hi, Bellamy. I hate to ask this on a weekend, but I have to deworm a herd of approximately nine hundred dairy goats, and the farmer is short-staffed. I could use a second set of hands to help measure and administer the meds, if you're available."

There is a long pause on the other end of the line.

"Bellamy?"

"One sec, Doc."

She covers the phone and speaks to someone in the background. All I hear is a mumbled conversation.

"Doc?"

"Still here," I assure her.

"I'm at Rustic Peak, but Elle says she and Walker can bring me to you when he gets done on the baler. He should be done in maybe fifteen minutes."

"That works. I have to swing by the office to get some supplies. They can drop you off there."

"Okay. See you shortly."

She disconnects the call.

I should have said something, anything, after last night instead of just getting straight to business. Truth is, I'm not sure what to say. I'm not sure what she expects or what I expect.

Shit.

It's been a long time since I had to try to decipher a woman's thoughts. I forgot how damn hard and uncomfortable that feat is.

Guess you'll just have to play it by ear, Haralson, and hope you don't fuck it up.

I'm in my office when the bell sounds up front.

Two seconds later, Walker's presence graces my door. "What's up, Doc?"

I look up at his amused face. "How long have you been waiting to use that one?" I ask.

"Forever, man. It just never felt right till now," he says.

My eyes move past him in search of Bellamy.

"She's over at the café, grabbing another coffee. She and Elle stayed up all night, gabbing, and they are both running on steam this morning," he tells me.

Damn, and here I am, dragging her into work unexpectedly.

I sit back in my chair and think.

"If she's not feeling up to it, I can do this myself. It'll just take longer, but I won't charge for the extra time."

"Nah, it ain't going to hurt her to see what it's like to tie one on and have to drag her ass up and to work anyway. We have to do it all the time."

"But she isn't supposed to work today," I note.

He shrugs. "She'll live. How are you doing today?" he asks.

I glance up and see genuine concern in his expression. "I'm good."

"You sure? If we need to have another one of those touchy-feely heart-to-hearts, we can. If that one didn't sink in well enough, I mean. We don't have them often, and we don't talk about them afterward, but if you need to be set straight again—"

"I'm good. Thanks," I cut him off when I hear the bell again.

He points his finger at me. "You'd better be. Or round two is going to happen," he warns.

"He'd better be what?" Bellamy's head peeks around his large frame and into the office.

"He'd better be ready to do shots with me tonight at the bonfire," he answers oddly.

"The bonfire?" I ask.

"Yep, at Myer's place. The girls are doing some Sippy thing over there, and we are tagging along and having moonshine by the moonlight."

"Sip and See. It's where we all come over to meet the baby and drink cocktails," Bellamy clarifies.

"Yeah, whatever the hell she said. It's just a fancy name for them to get together and fawn all over the new filly and get loaded."

"It kind of is. We don't usually plan them around here, but Sophie says they are all the rage in New York, and she threw it together. I swear, city people have a party for everything," she explains.

"So, are you in, Doc?" Walker raises his eyebrows at me.

"I, um, sure." I give in.

"Great! We need all the backup we can get to wrangle the hen-house once they start drinking and crying over whatever makes girls cry when they get together with babies."

Bellamy cocks her hip and glares at him. "We are not weepy females. You take that back."

"Correction: y'all weren't weepy females, but since Sophie got here and once the babies started coming, you guys have turned into a hormonal mosh pit. You know it. It's exhausting and a little terrifying at times," Walker declares.

For a moment, she looks like she is going to argue, and then she eases her posture.

"Maybe," she concedes in defeat.

They are funny. Their relationship is foreign to me. Sure, I had my college buddies, and Annie and I had a few neighborhood couple friends we would barbecue with now and then, but these people know each other on a different level. They can tease each other. Push each other's buttons and argue on a dime, but in the end, they have each other's backs, no matter what. I've never had friends like that. No one to take my back when I lost her. No one to keep me going—apart from Mom. I hope they realize how lucky they are.

"I'm ready if you are. I picked us up some coffee, and it's in the Rover," Bellamy interrupts my thoughts.

"I'd better get back before Braxton realizes I'm gone and has a hissy fit," Walker says as he turns and follows Bellamy to the door.

I grab my bag and keys and follow them.

"Does Braxton have hissy fits?" I ask Bellamy.

"Not normally, but if anyone can inspire one from him, it's Walker."

"Seven tonight, Doc. Don't forget. And come hungry. I'm throwing burgers on the grill," Walker yells as he hops in his truck and backs out.

"It's official. They've claimed you now," Bellamy says as we watch him drive out of sight.

"Claimed me?"

"Yep. They don't let too many newcomers in. I guess you passed the test," she teases as she walks backward toward the truck, wearing a grin.

"I'm honored," I call after her.

They've claimed me.

Twenty-Four

BELLAMY

I HAD NO IDEA HOW HARD BRANDT ACTUALLY WORKED.

I saw Dr. Sherrill out on the ranch my entire life, but he was just a grandfatherly figure who came out every now and again, checking an infected hoof or assisting in a struggling birth or spending branding day, vaccinating calves. He was in and out. I never accounted for the fact that Stoney Ridge was just one of the dozens of ranches in and around Poplar Falls. Then, there were countless farms and dairies. I never saw the endless stream of pet owners coming to the clinic or the late-night calls because of an injured animal or predator attack. I wasn't aware of Saturday morning emergency parasite treatments for a large herd. He is literally on call twenty-four seven. He definitely needs full-time help and not just from Miss Elaine.

It takes hours to finish up at Golden Mountain Dairy Farm. Brandt administers the medication after I calculate the dose based on each goat's weight. It is time-consuming, but when we are done and Brandt has me write up an invoice for him without adding time and a half for the weekend call, the relief on Mr. Franklin's face is priceless. He gives me a tight hug, and he shakes Brandt's hand and thanks him profusely. Gratitude and respect are written all over him as we say our good-byes.

I watch him as we pull out of the gate.

"You're a good man, Brandt Haralson."

He looks over at me. "Just doing my job."

I shake my head at him. "No, you did him a huge favor, and you didn't have to. He looked worried, and you helped him out."

He looks straight ahead as he explains, "It's the best thing about moving here from the city. Having my own practice gives me the ability to discern and read every situation. My office in Portland was owned by a medical conglomerate, and they were all about the bottom line. I got into this profession because I love animals and I want to help them. Turns out, I love people just as much, and I want to help them as well. My hands were tied before, and I watched humans go into debt, making sure their fur babies got the treatment they needed. It didn't have to be that way. Now, I can make that call."

He takes a deep breath and continues, "It's one of the reasons I haven't hired another staff member yet. I want to keep us out of the red, so I can keep my fees low for the struggling ranches and farms in Poplar Falls."

I reach over and take his hand. "Well, you don't have to pay me for today."

"That's not what I was saying, Bellamy. I'm going to pay you for your work."

"I know it wasn't, but I agree with you, and if you can work for free on a Saturday, so can I."

He shakes his head.

"I mean it, and I don't want any argument from you. However, you can buy me lunch, and we'll call it even. Deal?"

I can tell he doesn't like it, but he has the sense to know I am equally as stubborn and that he might as well give in.

"Yes, ma'am. Lunch it is."

We stop and eat on our way back to town. Neither of us brings up last night as we eat, but there is also no awkwardness between us. We fall into an easy conversation, and I tell him all about the ruse we are playing on Doreen in order to pull off the surprise. He fills me in on his telephone call with Miss Elaine and about her adventures in Oregon.

Before we know it, we've been sitting for hours, just talking.

"Yikes, Dallas is expecting me soon," I say as I look at my phone.

"I didn't mean to keep you so long. I can't believe the time," he muses.

"That's because I'm such great company," I tease.

"That has to be it," he agrees. "Tell you what. Why don't we swing by my place so I can change, and then I'll get you home and drive you to the party?"

"Sounds like a good plan to me, Doc."

Twenty-Five

BRANDT

WE STOP BY THE CLINIC SO THAT I CAN DROP OFF MY MEDICAL bag and change clothes.

I leave Bellamy waiting in my office while I run upstairs to the apartment and quickly freshen up.

When I make it back down, I find her standing in front of my bookcase, holding a framed photo.

I walk behind and look at it with her over her shoulder.

She is reading the inscription on the back.

Brandy and me, celebrating! Ross University School of Veterinary Medicine, Class of 2016.

"Brandy?" she asks.

"That's Annie and me. We met in college, at a coffee shop on campus. We were both waiting for our coffees. The barista had misspelled my name, and they kept calling out an order for Brandy. When I finally realized it was my latte, it was cold, and I was late for my next class and very annoyed. She was waiting behind me and thought it was hysterical. We ended up at a table, talking for hours that day. She called me Brandy from that moment on. The day the photo was taken, we were celebrating my acceptance into the veterinarian program at Ross and her new job with the City of Portland's Department of Human Services."

"Annie?"

"My wife. She died a few years ago."

"I'm so sorry," she says softly.

"Me too."

"A vet and a social worker. Pets and children. Sounds like you two were a match made in heaven."

"I thought so. She worked with teens in the foster care system. It was her passion to help them find placement with good families."

"What happened to her?"

I walk behind my desk, and she turns, still holding the photo to her chest.

"I shouldn't have asked. It's none of my business. I'm being a nosy female." She tries to let me off the hook.

I don't know why, but I want her to know.

"She was killed by a junkie, leaving a restaurant one night."

I hear her quick intake of breath. She carefully places the frame back on the shelf.

"Are you ready to go?" she asks, effectively changing the subject, and I'm grateful.

"Yes, ma'am."

I drive her home, so she can shower and change.

I'm waiting with Mrs. Wilson on the porch, explaining that I offered to be her ride to the Sippy thing so she could drink and enjoy herself, when Winston and Myer come up from the barn.

"You two want some lemonade?" she offers them.

"Nah, I'm heading out to go help Dallas with Beau and Faith, so she can get ready for tonight," Myer informs her.

"Oh, wonderful. Brandt here is escorting your sister to the party," she says with a huge smile on her face.

Myer's eyes come to mine. "Glad you're joining us, Doc. Dallas has been cooped up for weeks now, and she is bursting with excitement that everyone is coming by. She'll be pleased to see you," he says.

"Thanks for the invite. Although I think it was Walker who extended the invitation without your knowledge."

"You don't need an invite. You're always welcome to anything we have at the house," he insists.

"Of course you are," Mrs. Wilson chimes in.

Winston just winks at me as he sits beside his wife, and she pours him a glass of lemonade.

"I'm off." Myer gives a little salute and takes off toward the driveway.

I feel awkward as hell, standing here with Bellamy's parents, waiting for her to get ready. It's like I'm a teenager, coming to pick up my date for the prom. My hands are just as sweaty.

"Relax, Doc. Take a load off. Bells is going to take a while to get ready. I don't know why, but it takes women three times as long to pull on clothes and shoes as it does us. It's baffling," Winston instructs, and I take a seat in one of the rockers opposite them.

"I received a telephone call from your mother last night," Mrs. Wilson tells me. "She's really enjoying her time with the grandkids, but she is ready to come home. She says the sounds of the city and all the ornery folks are driving her mad."

"I reckon she has assimilated to mountain life," I comment.

"She has. Plus, she misses bingo night and the ladies' auxiliary meetings. I think she plans to join the church when she gets back," she fills me in.

"She certainly does seem to enjoy the fellowship," I agree.

"And we enjoy her." She beams.

I'm so happy Mom has found peace and happiness here. I felt selfish, dragging her away from everyone she knew to move here with me, but she insisted that she come along when I told her I was moving.

"Your sister has Wes and the kids and your cousins here. She'll be fine. I'm coming along to make sure you are fine. Besides, I could use a change of scenery myself, and I hear the Colorado Mountains are divine. If I don't like it there, I'll just move back in a year."

I guess she has decided to stay after all.

"Bellamy tells me you purchased the Sugarman Homestead," Beverly continues.

"Yes, ma'am."

She whistles. "It's a lovely place, but it is definitely going to need a lot of work," she utters.

"I'm sure you are telling the boy something he already knows, Bev," Winston interjects.

"Oh, you hush. I'm just making small talk."

"You're just being nosy," he corrects.

"I am not," she snaps.

"She is," he says to me.

I decide to go ahead and spill, so they don't argue. "It is going to be a project, but I'm looking forward to it. Bellamy actually helped me get started, tearing out some of the old cabinetry. Contractors begin the remodel in the kitchen this week. Hopefully, that part will be done by the time Mom gets back."

"Bellamy is helping, you say?" Her question is laced with curiosity.

"I don't know if she wants to do anything else, but she was great at tearing things up."

Winston lets out a guttural laugh. "She always has been a little female wrecking ball," he muses.

"I'm sure she'll love to keep helping. She's always adored that house," Mrs. Wilson adds.

"I think you've made your point, dear. No need to keep pushing and scare the boy off," Winston advises.

"I don't know what in the devil you're going on about," she says to him, exasperated.

He looks at me and rolls his eyes. "Sure you don't, dear."

She opens her mouth, preparing to hurl her retort, when the door swings open and Bellamy appears.

She is wearing a blue-and-white gingham halter-top romper with navy sandals. Her hair is curled and flowing down her back. And a pair of sunglasses are shoved haphazardly on her head.

She looks like a summer day.

"Ready, Doc? Dallas just texted and asked if we could stop in town and grab a couple more bottles of wine. Apparently, Myer didn't pick up nearly enough."

I stand. "Ready if you are. Thank you for the lemonade, Mrs. Wilson."

She stands as well and wraps me in a hug. "Oh, it was my pleasure, and you call me Beverly, you hear. No more of this Mrs. Wilson nonsense," she demands.

"Yes, ma'am."

I shake Winston's hand as she hugs Bellamy.

"I'll be waiting to carry her in," he whispers loudly to me.

"Pop! I heard that." She feigns offense.

"Wasn't trying to keep you from hearing it, sweetheart."

He smiles lovingly at his daughter, and she kisses his cheek.

Then, I walk her to my truck, and we head to town.

Twenty-Six

BELLAMY

B
RANDT AND I RIDE IN SILENCE TO MY BROTHER'S CABIN. IT'S NOT exactly awkward, but it's obvious neither of us knows what to say about what happened last night. At least he isn't avoiding me, so I guess that's a good sign.

When we make it to the party, he immediately joins the boys outside at the horseshoe pits while I take the wine inside.

Sophie, Elle, and Silas's wife, Chloe, are already set up on the living room floor with Faith lying on a blanket.

"Bells, it's about time you arrived. We're almost out of wine," Dallas says from the couch. Empty wineglass in hand.

"Since when do you drink wine?" I ask what I think is a fair question.

She looks down at her glass and frowns. "I thought if I limited myself to wine, I wouldn't get too drunk. I don't want to pass out and not hear Faith when she wakes up to feed," she grumbles.

"I thought that you pumped, so you could drink. Doesn't that mean Myer can get up and feed her?" Sophie asks.

"I did. But I like getting up with her. And he has to get up at the ass-crack of dawn every day, so I like for him to get extra sleep on Sundays."

"You know, I heard him talking to Momma the other day, and I think he's a little bit jealous that you're the only one who can get up with her and feed her. He really wants some quiet one-on-one time with her," I tell her, only slightly exaggerating the conversation.

"Really?" she asks.

"Yep. He wants extra daddy-daughter bonding time. You don't want to rob him of that, do you?"

She eyes me suspiciously. "I'm going to pretend you aren't trying to manipulate a new mother and that all of that's true. Now, hand me a beer out of the fridge, please."

I set the wine bottles down and grab us both a cold one before rejoining them.

"How did you get down there?" I ask Sophie as she lies beside the baby, propped up on an elbow.

"Very carefully, and I think I live here now because I don't believe I'm going to be able to get myself up," she groans.

Dallas pops the top and takes a long pull. "Ahh, that's so good," she exclaims.

"I miss wine." Sophie pouts.

"I bought you some sparkling grape juice, so you could pretend," Dallas offers.

Sophie wrinkles her nose at that.

"I brought you some strawberry ice cream and churros," Elle counters.

"Ding, ding, ding! We have a winner," Sophie declares.

"Such a weird combination," I muse.

"Don't knock it till you've tried it. It will change your life!" Sophie insists.

The door opens, and Walker's head pops in.

"Cheese on all the burgers?" he asks.

All of us nod.

He gives us a salute and shuts the door.

"Where's Sonia?" I ask.

"She called earlier. She and Ricky got in an argument because he wanted her to go to his best friend's house to watch the fights with him and his wife. She wanted to come here. They finally compromised and are going to swing by here on their way there. So, they'll be here shortly," Elle explains.

"Well, that's progress, I guess."

"If you say so."

Elle obviously disagrees, but we made a pact to keep our opinions to ourselves when it comes to Ricky unless Sonia asks for them. Which she doesn't often.

"Bye," Dallas says as she hugs me for the fourth time.

"Bye, sis. I'll see you tomorrow at Sunday dinner," I remind her.

She hiccups. "Yep, we'll be there," she confirms.

Walker tries to squeeze by us, and she nabs him and forces a hug on him.

"Woman, you are tanked," he accuses.

"Am not," she argues.

"She hasn't drunk anything in close to a year. I think the beer hit her hard," Sophie tattles.

Dallas sticks her tongue out at her best friend. "Narc," she accuses.

Sophie laughs and wraps her arms around Dallas's neck. "I love you," she says.

"I love you too," a disgruntled Dallas returns.

She leans down and puts her lips to Sophie's belly. "Auntie Dallas loves you too, Lily Claire." She kisses the bump.

Myer comes up behind Dallas, snakes an arm around her waist, and pulls her into his chest.

"Everyone has to go, sweetheart. It's getting late," he whispers into her hair.

"I think that's our cue," Brandt says from behind me.

Dallas leans in and whispers, "He just wants drunken sex. The doctor gave us the thumbs-up yesterday."

"Hell, man, why didn't you say so? Everybody, to your vehicles and vacate the property immediately!" Walker shouts.

Myer laughs and shakes his head. "Thanks, man."

"I always have your six, bud. Enjoy all the sloppy lovin'."

Walker leads Elle to the driveway, and we all follow suit.

Elle eyes Brandt as we stop at his truck.

"You two have a good night," she says before she walks off.

Walker slaps him on the back. "Yep. Have a good one, Doc. You're one hell of a horseshoe partner."

Braxton loads Sophie and then calls out before he gets in the truck, "We'll be around about noon, Brandt."

"That's right. Noon, sir," Walker agrees.

I look over at Brandt in question.

"They are coming to assist in stripping and sanding the floors tomorrow." He says it like he can't believe they would want to help him.

"That's great. Three sets of hands are better than one."

He opens the door and helps me inside. We are once again alone and silent. I reach and turn on the radio.

"I had fun tonight," he mutters as I search for a station.

"Yeah, me too," I agree.

"You want to ride around for a while?" he asks. "I mean, unless you're tired," he adds.

"Not ready for the night to end, Doc?"

He purses his lips together.

"Not ready for sleep," he answers oddly.

I finally find the country station I like and turn the music up. I kick off my sandals and prop my feet on the dash.

"Then, let's cruise some back roads," I tell him.

He looks at me and smiles. Then, he pushes the button to lower both our windows, and the truck fills with the cool, fresh breeze.

I lay my head back against the seat and close my eyes while Granger Smith's voice drifts through the air.

At some point, Brandt's arm comes up to rest on the back of the seat, and he starts to absentmindedly play with my hair. Twirling it around his fingers.

I moan and loll my head to the side to give him better access.

He looks over at me. "You like that?" he asks.

"Every girl likes having her hair played with," I inform him.

He looks back at the road, but his hand entangles deeper in my hair, and he starts to massage my scalp.

I close my eyes and begin to drift off.

"Bells," he calls.

"Hmm?"

"I enjoyed kissing you."

I try to rally and respond, but all I manage is a weak smile and a muttered, "I liked kissing you too."

He gently tugs my neck, and I let him pull me closer to him. I open one eye as I wrap an arm around his waist, lay my head on his shoulder, and snuggle in.

He continues to drive while I sleep.

When he pulls up to my house and turns off the ignition, it rouses me. I sit up and rub my eyes, and then I look at the clock on the dash. Hours. He drove around with me asleep, curled up to him, for hours.

My arm is still around him, and I bunch his shirt into my fist at his side as I try to stretch the sleep away.

"You're home," he whispers into my hair.

I drop my forehead to his chin. And his hand comes down and starts lazily rubbing up and down my back as he holds me.

"It's been a long time since I've had any kind of intimate touch," he confesses into the dark cab.

That makes me press closer into him.

"I forgot how good it feels to share the same space with another person. To hold a woman as she sleeps," he continues.

I lift my head and give him my eyes.

His bore into mine, and then they drop to my mouth.

He brings his hand back to my hair and wraps it in his fist.

Then, he guides my mouth to his.

This kiss is different than before. It's slow and sweet, but I feel it all the way to my toes … an ache. I want to wrap myself around him.

I can tell he is close to losing control, too, as he tugs me as near to him as possible in the small space. My hand finds his thigh. I dig my nails into his muscle, and he groans.

That's when the porch light blinks on.

I pull away and look over my shoulder at my daddy in his pajama pants, standing at the door like he did when I was a teenager.

I look back at Brandt's wide eyes.

"My daddy just caught us making out in the driveway," I whisper.

He presses his lips together, trying to hold back a laugh.

I sit up and reach for the door handle, and he grabs my hand and squeezes.

"I'll get your door," he says.

"That's okay. I got it this time."

"Sweet dreams, Bells."

"Night, Doc."

I hop down and shut the door. I walk backward to the house and watch as he backs out and heads up toward the gate.

Pop meets me at the steps.

"I think I'm in trouble, Pop," I say without turning around.

His big hand lands on my shoulder. "I think maybe he's the one in trouble, sweetheart," he mutters.

Twenty-Seven

BRANDT

"DOES THIS OUTLET HAVE POWER?" WALKER ASKS AS HE tries to start the floor sander he plugged into the extension cord across from the kitchen.

"They all should. The power company came out Friday morning to check the wiring and turn on the electricity."

He tries again, and still, nothing.

"Brax, when did we use this thing last?"

Braxton is in the dining room, applying a coat of liquid paint thinner.

He removes his mask and answers, "We used it upstairs at your place last weekend. It should work fine."

Walker goes and checks the connection again. "Dammit, I'm not getting anything. The thing is dead."

Braxton props the handle to the roller against the wall and walks into the kitchen. He flips the switch under the old mounted telephone, and the sander hums to life. Then, he marches back to the dining room.

"You could have just told me what to do, jackass," Walker calls.

Braxton extends his arm behind his back and gives him the finger.

They showed up at noon sharp this afternoon with a truck bed full of equipment. Equipment I would have had to pay for in order to get the job done.

When we had been sitting around the fire, eating our burgers last night, Myer had asked what my plans were for today, and I told them I was starting the floors as long as Bramble Building Materials was open on Sunday to rent what I needed. I had intended to pick everything up on Saturday before Hal Franklin called about his sick goats. Braxton had asked what all I needed and said he had everything, so he'd offered his help, and Walker had stepped up next.

The three of us work steadily for the next few hours before stopping to eat sandwiches Sophie sent with Braxton.

"I think we have enough edging tape to finish up the kitchen and dining room before we call it a day. That way, your floors are ready when they arrive with your island and cabinets tomorrow," Braxton says as we sit on the tailgate of his truck.

"I appreciate all your help today, guys. I couldn't have finished a single room on my own," I tell them.

"We would have helped you sooner if we'd known you were tearing everything out yourself. The demo is Walker's favorite part of any project. Tearing things up is his special talent."

Walker doesn't disagree. He just smiles around a mouthful.

"Bellamy helped with that part," I tell them.

"Bellamy?" Walker asks.

I laugh. "Yeah, you should have seen her with the sledgehammer, ready to start whacking away at the counters. I had to pry it out of her hand. She was going to hurt herself for sure."

"That woman is stronger than you think. She once got so mad at Myer and me that she picked up a ten-gallon bucket of WaterSeal and chucked it at us. Those damn things are heavy. Hurt like hell too," Walker tells us.

"Yeah, these ranch girls aren't like the girls in the city. They aren't afraid of hard work. But I wouldn't let Sophie or Elle handle a sledgehammer either if I were around," Braxton agrees.

"You and Bells looked like you were in a good place last night," Walker says.

"We are. I think."

"You're really into her, huh?" he adds.

"Yeah, I'm into her," I admit.

"Well, just remember, she's Myer's little sister and Elle's best friend, so if you break her heart, I will have to break your kneecaps," Walker states.

"I, uh …"

"He's kidding. Fuck, Walk. He doesn't know you well enough yet. Stop being a dick," Braxton scolds.

"Who says I'm kidding?" Walker asks.

"I have no intention of hurting her," I tell him.

"Yeah, well, sometimes, shit goes down, even when you have the best of intentions," he says, and it sounds like he speaks from experience.

"That's enough yapping. Let's get back to work," Braxton orders.

Walker slides his eyes to me. "I don't know why he always gets to be in charge," he whines.

"Because if you were in charge, we'd never get anything done," Braxton throws over his shoulder. "Now, stop feeding your face and come on."

Walker begrudgingly throws the rest of his third sandwich back in the paper sack and follows Braxton.

"They look good!" Braxton admires as I pull up the last of the tape.

We stripped, sanded, and stained the hardwood a dark espresso, and he is right; they look better than I imagined. I intended to stain them a golden-wheat color, which was closer to the original floors, but Bellamy talked me into the dark hue because she thought it would look better with the gray-quartz countertops and black cabinetry I'd picked out.

"They do. This kitchen is going to be kick-ass when you're finished," Walker agrees.

"Are you planning on keeping that fireplace in the dining room?" Braxton asks.

"I am. Bellamy thinks I should paint the brick white and add a dark mantel that matches the cabinets in the kitchen."

He nods his head. "She's right. That would look amazing."

"And what does Miss Wilson think you should do in here?" Walker asks from the living room.

"A dark gray accent wall and remote blinds," I answer.

He looks around and back to me. "There aren't any windows in here," he says.

"Right, and add floor-to-ceiling windows to let the natural light in," I add.

"Oh, is that all?" he asks.

Braxton laughs.

"This is your house, man. Don't let her female all over it before you even get a chance to move in," Walker protests.

"Says the man who literally calls Elle to ask her opinion of where he should add a damn nail to a support beam," Braxton teases.

"Do not make me say it, man. Don't," Walker warns as he points at Braxton.

"Say what?"

Walker looks at me. "She uses sexual persuasion to bribe me into getting exactly what she wants. What can I say? I'm a weak man when it comes to that woman," he says.

"Fuck, Walk, really?" Braxton stomps off to the door.

"I tried to warn you," Walker yells after him.

We pack up and help Braxton get everything back into his truck.

"I'd leave this stuff here for you, but we need it over at Walk's this week. I'll bring it back next Sunday though to help you do the rest of the downstairs. If we have time, we'll get to the second floor too," Braxton says before shutting the tailgate.

"Can I pay you guys for your time?" I ask.

Braxton shakes his head. "No, pitching in is part of being

neighbors and friends around here. I'm sure Sophie will want a studio or something eventually, and you can come to help me."

"What about you, Walker? Need any help at your place this week?" I ask.

"I can always use an extra set of hands. We want to get that place done before Sophie bursts and Braxton is rendered useless for six weeks or longer," he says.

"Then, I will be there after work tomorrow," I tell him.

He claps me on the back. "Make it Tuesday or Wednesday, Doc. You'll want to come here after work tomorrow to check out your new kitchen and enjoy it. The work will be there at my place all week long."

"You've got yourself a deal," I say. I thank them both again before they drive off.

I turn to look at the house. The white paint is chipping and peeling, and it needs a fresh coat, but I think I'm going to give it a bit of a face-lift and change it to a colonial blue with white trim and black shutters and doors. Still regal but more me.

It's coming together nicely.

It's becoming home.

Twenty-Eight

BRANDT

"DOC, ARE YOU IN HERE?"

I'm upstairs, pulling up the carpet, when I hear her voice calling from below.

"Bellamy? I'm up here."

The click of her boots on marble echoes in the hall as she climbs the steps.

She stops when she reaches the landing and watches me as I rip the last piece of carpet loose from the baseboard in the hallway leading to the spare rooms.

"The floors downstairs are gorgeous," she says as she assesses the mess around me.

I stand in nothing but my jeans. I got hot up here and shed the shirt and boots about halfway through.

Her eyes travel from my shoulders, down my chest, and to my bare feet. Then, she looks around and turns toward the master bedroom.

I follow as she clicks on the light. A large California king-size bed stands against the far end of the room, and the wall between this room and the one beside it is gone. As is the one to the bath. She walks inside and spins.

"It feels so much larger in here already. Even with this monster of a bed."

"The other furniture is in the bedroom down the hall until they get the closets framed in and the bath extended, but at least now, if I'm working here late and I'm too tired to drive back to the apartment, I have a place to crash."

"Good thinking," she approves.

"I didn't know you were coming by," I say as she sits on the end of the bed and bounces.

"Momma sent you some leftovers from supper. We thought you might have gotten too caught up on working to stop and eat anything today."

She brings her eyes to mine.

"You look like you're exhausted," she observes.

I wipe the back of my neck with a towel I hung on the banister earlier.

"Just hot," I complain. "The AC unit was installed, but they didn't get the thermostat in, so it was a hundred degrees up here. I installed it myself about thirty minutes ago, but it's going to take a while for it to catch up and get the house cooled down."

She wrinkles her nose, and then her eyes start dancing as she says, "I have an idea."

She leads me down to the back door.

"We can go for a swim to cool off," she says as she kicks off her boots and starts for the woods.

I follow her toward the sound of the water.

Just as we make it into the tree line, the river comes into view. Water rushes down a wall of rocks and into a pool.

"I knew it. This is the cove we used to swim in all the time when we were kids. I thought it backed up to here," she says.

She walks to the edge and toes the water.

"Perfect," she breathes.

"It's dirty," is all I manage to choke out as I watch her reach up and remove the band from her hair and shake the long locks free.

"It's mountain water. Fed into the stream right off the rocks. There's nothing dirty about it," she says.

She turns to face me and grabs the hem of her tee. She lifts it above her head and drops it at her bare feet.

"Come on, Doc. Find your wild."

It's a dare.

She stands there with her back to the river, slowly stripping each piece of clothing off until she is down to nothing but her bra and panties. I watch in rapt fascination as she reaches behind herself and undoes the bra, letting the straps fall from her shoulders. She tosses it to the side, and I get a brief glimpse of her beautiful breasts before she covers them with one arm. I look up, and her face has a mischievous grin. She extends the other arm and curls her finger, beckoning me to her.

I hesitate only a moment, taking in the gorgeous creature before me—from her red-tipped toes; up her long, sexy, tanned legs; and to those hips covered by a sliver of white lace. I start moving forward without thinking. Undoing the button of my jeans as I give chase. Her eyes brighten in excitement, and she squeals before she turns and takes off running to the water before diving in. I've made it to the edge by the time she surfaces, and she smooths her long, wet hair from her face. I grip my jeans and tug them to my ankles. Heat dances in her eyes as she takes in my nakedness.

She turns and starts to swim out farther, and I race in after her.

I catch up to her in minutes, and she splashes me in the face as I make it to her and clasp her waist. She struggles to kick past me, but I have a firm grip on her. Finally, she settles and snakes her arms around my shoulders. Her fingers find the hair at the nape of my neck.

"Gotcha," I claim as I pull her tight.

She brings her eyes to mine, and that mischievous dimple peeks out of her right cheek.

"So, what are you going to do with me?" she asks.

Another dare.

I take a huge step, moving us forward. She instinctively wraps her legs around my waist as we reach a depth that is over her head but not mine.

The lace of her panties brushes my growing cock, and that's all it takes to bring it to full attention. I know she feels it when her eyes widen slightly and her lips part. Her tongue darts out nervously, and her breath quickens.

I bury my nose into her neck, just below her ear, and I inhale deeply. She sighs and relaxes her body into me, bringing her chin to my shoulder. I hold her as the water laps around us.

I place a kiss on her collarbone, and she throws her head back to give me better access, which causes her breasts to peek out of the water. I cup one with my hand and gently knead it. She closes her eyes and moans, bowing her back and bringing the pink tip closer to my face. I suck it between my teeth and give it a rough tug. She bucks, and I release it and lick and blow across it. It tightens to a hard peak, and I wrap my lips around it once more. Her hips start to rock into mine, and as soon as she finds the contact she is searching for, she quickens her movement. Her heat feels so good, sliding up and down my aching erection.

I slide my mouth to the other breast and give it attention as she continues to glide against my eager cock. When I can take no more, I bite down on her nipple, and she gasps and raises her head. I slide my hands around her back and to her ass. I hoist her up, bringing her closer.

"Give me your mouth, Bellamy," I command.

She clasps her arms tighter around me and does just that.

Fuck, she tastes good.

I take all of her weight as she loses herself to pleasure again. I feel her body begin to tremble and find her clit in the water. I circle it with my thumb, using the lace of her panties to create even more friction as she moves more urgently.

Her legs tighten around me, and she begins to shudder as she gets closer. I release her mouth so that I can watch as she finally shatters. Her cries float into the air, echoing around us.

It's the most beautiful thing I've ever heard.

Twenty-Nine

BELLAMY

He holds me in the water until my trembling stops. He's breathing heavily, and I'm clinging to him.

I finally bring my face from his neck and look at him. His expression is soft.

"Are you cooler now?" I ask.

He grins. "Not exactly," he answers.

I let go, and he releases me. I kick my legs, and I swim a couple of feet away before looking back at him.

"Come on. The water gets colder, the farther you go in." I beckon him.

He stands there, and a painful expression crosses his face. "I'm going to need a minute," he says.

I start back toward him, and he puts his hand up to halt me.

"That's not going to help. You need to stay over there," he states firmly.

He must see my face fall at his demand because he gives me a tight smile and explains, "I need a minute, sweetheart, and you coming back over here at this moment is going to make that minute even longer."

It takes me a second, but then I get it.

"Oh," I murmur, and a pang of guilt hits me because my limbs are loose and sated.

I swim to him anyway, and he watches me as I approach.

"I've heard a cold shower helps with that," I tease.

"Have you now?" he asks with amusement in his voice.

I nod.

"In fact, I think we should test that theory," I suggest before kicking past him and walking up onto the shore.

I pick up my bra, jeans, and my tee as I walk back toward the house.

I look over my shoulder, and he is slowly making his way to the edge of the water.

"I'll be waiting for you," I tell him before taking off for the house at a jog.

I run upstairs, step into the massive glass shower, and turn on the sprays. There are four. A rain showerhead in the center and one spray coming from each of the three walls. I slide my panties down my legs and kick them off, and then I stand in the middle with my back to the glass door.

I don't turn around as I hear him enter the bathroom.

He stands there for a while, just watching me as I take the shampoo and lather it in my hair.

"Are you coming in?" I ask over my shoulder.

The shower door opens, but he hesitates.

I keep my feet planted and stop myself from turning around.

Finally, I feel his heat at my back … and then his lips at my ear.

"This isn't a cold shower," he growls.

Under the waterfall, I lean my head back onto his chest. I blink up at him as the soap rinses out of my hair and glides down our bodies.

"It can be. If that's what you want."

He reaches around me for the knob, and disappointment washes over me as I watch him slowly begin to turn it.

I close my eyes and start to pull away when the spray gradually gets warmer.

"Where are you going?" he asks as he moves my hair and touches his lips to my shoulder.

I open my eyes to a cloud of steam licking its way up the tiles.

His hands rest on my hips as he pulls me back into him. He slips them around my stomach as he starts to gently suck at my throat.

A whimper escapes me as he continues to explore my bare skin.

He strokes the underside of my breasts before taking their weight into his palms. My knees grow weak as the pads of his thumbs find my taut nipples.

"Brandt," I moan his name as I sink further back into him.

"Does that feel good, baby?" he asks as he rolls the tender peaks between his fingers.

"Yes … ah," I groan.

He feeds one of his knees between my legs to steady me, and the contact sends a shudder through me.

I reach out to the tiles for support and bear down on him to get better pressure where I want it. It feels so damn good. A needy sound rises in my throat, and then all of a sudden, Brandt picks me up and spins me around. My back hits the shower wall, and his mouth covers mine.

His control finally snaps, and his kiss grows wild. His teeth sink into my bottom lip, and I gasp. He takes the opportunity to hungrily suck my tongue into his mouth. I wrap my arms around his neck and tug at his wet hair. I can't get him close enough.

He tears his mouth from mine, and the heat in his eyes sears me as they move down my body like a physical touch. His hands begin kneading my swollen breasts again, and I lean my head back. His mouth finds the curve of my neck and kisses a trail down my collarbone. I close my eyes and just feel as his teeth graze one of my nipples. I throw my arms out wide and brace myself on the wall. He sucks it into his mouth and begins to pull at the other. Heat pools in my belly as one of his hands moves up the inside of my thigh.

I cry out at his touch when his fingertips find my swollen entrance.

His mouth releases my nipple, and his head comes up to look at my face as I tremble. His forehead comes to mine as he sticks a finger inside of me.

"Fuck, Bellamy, you're so ready for me."

I grab his shoulders as he adds a second finger.

"So wet," he murmurs as he buries his head in my neck. His breathing erratic.

"Please," I beg as I sink my nails into his skin. I'm not even sure what I'm pleading for. I just need more. More of him.

"I need to taste you," he says as he pulls away and then goes to a knee.

He kisses a path from my breast and down my stomach as he continues to slowly pump his fingers in and out of me.

When his mouth reaches his fingers, he spreads me open, and his tongue darts out and licks me. A jolt of electricity climbs up my spine as he sucks my clit deep.

He tugs one of my legs over his shoulder to give himself better access. He presses my stomach against the wall and holds me steady before he buries his face in my heat and starts to lap at me like a starving man. I grab his hair and hold him where I want him. Where I need him.

His tongue finds my opening, and he starts to thrust in and out while his thumb runs circles over my clit. I bring my hips up and down, moving to meet him. My hands in his hair hold him in place as I ride his tongue. I'm so close. He pinches my clit and I fall over the cliff.

One minute, I'm screaming his name as I come, and the next, I'm being lifted and hoisted up and out of the shower. He drops me on the counter beside the sink, and he grasps my legs and brings them up on the edge. My knees fall to the sides, opening me wide to him.

"So damn beautiful," he says before he takes his cock in his hand and brings the tip to my entrance. He slides it through my folds, coating it in my wetness. Then, he releases it and grabs the ledge of the counter before pushing into me fully.

I groan and then whisper, "You feel so good inside of me."

It's like my words flip a switch. He lets out a growl and grabs my hips. Then, he pulls out and buries himself back inside me. I rise to meet his thrusts as his rhythm quickens. I know my body is climbing again, and I want more. More of his mouth on mine, more of his skin against mine, just more everything.

My legs start to shake uncontrollably as I come undone again. I can tell he's holding on by a thread, and as my body ignites, I start to spasm around him. He closes his eyes, and his head flies back as he pumps his release inside of me.

Once we both come down, he brings his eyes to mine. Still inside of me, he leans in and tenderly kisses my lips before he slides out. He grabs a hand towel from the hook beside us. Turns on the water in the sink and then gently cleans me up.

He lifts me in his arms without saying a word. He walks me into the bedroom and lays me down. He covers me with the down comforter and tucks me in, and then he turns to walk away. I reach for his hand, and he looks back at me and smiles.

"I have to turn the water off in the shower. I'll be right back."

I let him go, and he walks back to the bathroom.

I snuggle deep into the soft covers and close my eyes.

Seconds later, I feel the rustle of the blanket and then his heat at my back. He snakes an arm around my waist and pulls me back into him. His face buries in my hair, and his warm breath against my neck lulls me to sleep.

Thirty

BRANDT

THE SOUND OF A BIRD CHIRPING ROUSES ME. I OPEN ONE EYE and am blinded by light pouring in from the window. Confused, I feel for my phone, but there is no nightstand. I try to open my eyes again and realize I'm in the new house. The offending window is one I haven't had a chance to cover yet.

Jeez, what time is it?

I move to get up, but my progress is halted by the arm wrapped around my waist. I look down, and a mess of blonde hair is snuggled up under the crook of my arm. Bellamy's face is in my side, puffs of her even, warm breath bathing my pec.

Last night returns to me in a flash as my gaze runs up the length of her bare legs, which are twisted in the sheets, to the roundness of her hips and up to the swell of her breasts pressed against me.

My cock reacts to the memory of being buried inside her as her body milked my orgasm.

I try to slide out from under her without disturbing her sleep, but her arm tightens on me, and she murmurs something unintelligible into my side.

"Good morning," I say as I run my fingers through her tangled locks.

"Mmm."

All of a sudden, it hits me. The bright sunshine.

Shit.

I jolt up, and it startles her.

She comes up on an elbow and blinks. "What's wrong?"

I race to the bathroom in search of my jeans. I nab them off the floor and pull them on. Then, I glance back out at her. Her messy, confused look is adorable, and I'd love to go back and kiss her fully awake, but I can't.

"It's Monday morning. I have no idea what time it is, but it's late morning," I tell her.

She sits there for a moment, and then it hits her.

"Oh no," she shrieks as she kicks the sheets away and bolts up.

"Do you remember who our first appointment is?" I ask as I try to remember where I removed my shirt.

The spare room. Pulling carpet. Right.

Her eyes fly to mine. "Cowboy!"

Great. Her fucking brother. What are the odds? How the hell am I supposed to explain this to Myer?

She runs into the bathroom and comes out in her cutoff shorts and tank.

"I can't go to work in this," she says in a panic.

I leave her to her meltdown and jog to the other room to retrieve my tee. It smells like a gym bag from the dried sweat as I pull it over my head.

We collide in the hallway as we both race to the stairs.

I grab her shoulders to steady her.

Then, I look down at the two of us, and I burst into roaring laughter. She watches me like I've lost my mind, and that makes me laugh harder.

"Pull it together, Doc," she demands.

I bend over, shaking with laughter till I can't breathe.

She steps back and plants a hand on her hip. "This isn't funny," she bites.

I bring my tear-filled eyes to her annoyed ones. She waits for me to finally catch my breath.

"I feel like a teenager, getting caught by his parents. I haven't felt that way in a long time."

Her expression softens, and she shakes her head. "Me neither."

I walk over and kiss her forehead.

"I'll call Myer. You head home and get ready. Come in as soon as you can. I'll fumble my way through until you make it," I say against her skin.

She fists my shirt back and sighs. Then, she pulls back and looks up at me. "You stink, Doc."

That causes me to break down in laughter again as I lead her down the stairs and out to our trucks.

I slept in. I haven't slept in, in years. Not once. The last thing I remember is pulling Bellamy into my arms and the sound of her breaths growing heavy and even. Then, nothing. No dreams. No waking in the middle of the night in a cold sweat. Nothing until that bird sang me awake.

When I get my cell phone charged on the way into town, I have four missed calls from Myer. He is not amused when he answers my call back. He took time off from the ranch to run home and get Beau's dog to bring him in for his shots, so Dallas wouldn't have to load the baby, Beau, and pup all up to bring him herself. Now, he has to get back to work and can't wait any longer.

His frustration is warranted.

I explain that I passed out at the new house after working all day. I hadn't meant to stay there, so I didn't have an alarm set or a change of clothes. I apologize profusely and offer to come by his house this weekend and vaccinate Cowboy.

That appeases him. He says he has some paper in his truck and offers to scratch a note down and put it on the door for me, letting others know I will be in shortly.

Then, he asks, "Why isn't Bells here?"

My mind goes completely blank, and all words fly from my head. "Doc?"

Then, a chuckle comes over the line.

"Right. See you this weekend."

Then, he hangs up.

I shoot Bellamy a warning text before I run upstairs to comfort a very put out Lou-Lou and jump in the shower. Myer is surely going to make it back to Stoney Ridge before she can escape.

I get dressed quickly and run down to open the office. I stop dead when I see my mother standing there, looking at Myer's sign in her hand. She looks up at me with confusion, and quirks an eyebrow at me in question.

"Mom, I didn't expect you back until Thursday," I say.

"I was ready to come home. So, I caught an earlier flight. Doreen picked me up this morning."

"I would have come to get you," I say as I round the desk and embrace her. Happy to see her.

"Well, I thought you would be hard at work, so I called and asked if she could come get me at the airport."

"I slept late," I only half-fib.

She looks at me in surprise.

"I know. I'm shocked too."

"Where's Bellamy?" she asks.

There it is again.

I shrug.

"She isn't here yet, so she must have slept late too."

I know that sounds nonsensical, but it's all I've got.

Her perceptive eyes come to me, and she starts to speak. Thankfully, the bell above the door chimes, and our ten o'clock appointment walks in, saving me from any further explanation.

For the moment at least.

Thirty-One

BELLAMY

I DRESS AS FAST AS I CAN AND COME SKIDDING TO A HALT IN THE LIVING room when Myer walks through the front door with Cowboy on his heels.

Uh-oh.

I turn to go out the back when his voice stops me.

"Good morning, Bells—or should I say, good afternoon?"

I slowly turn to face him. He has a hip propped against the island and a shit-eating grin on his face.

"Hey."

Cowboy trots up to me and barks a greeting as well. Then, he plants his paws on my thigh and stands there with his tongue out and tail wagging, waiting for my affection.

"Good morning to you too, Cowboy," I coo as I scratch between his ears, and he closes his eyes, pulling his head to the side in puppy ecstasy.

"I'd be careful. He missed his vaccination this morning, so if he nips at you and you start foaming at the mouth later, it's not my fault," Myer states just as Momma comes in from her Monday morning breakfast date with Dottie.

"There's no way he has rabies just because you missed his vaccination appointment, Myer," she says as she brushes past him and bends to pet the dog.

He quickly abandons me and follows Momma to the counter, where she opens a treat jar and tosses him three.

"Momma, we give him treats when he goes outside to potty, and he only gets one, not a handful," Myer gripes.

"That's the rule at your house, not at Grandma's house. At Grandma's house, you get treats whenever Grandma wants to give them, and you get as many as she wants to give you."

Cowboy looks at Myer and barks, as if to say, *Yeah, what she said.*

"Rotten kids and rotten dogs—that's what we're going to have," Myer mumbles at the pup.

I take the opportunity to try to make my escape out the door.

"Bellamy, why are you home at ten, dear? Shouldn't you be at work?"

"Um ..." I start.

"She overslept. I showed up and woke her up," Myer lies.

I mouth, *Thank you*, to him.

Momma looks confused. "I thought your truck was gone when I left this morning."

"You must have missed it." I shrug. "Well, I'm late. See you later. Love you both."

I rush out the door, and Cowboy starts barking and runs to the screen.

"I love you too, Cowboy," I yell as I hop in my truck and get gone before anyone else can ask me any more questions.

I walk in and drop my purse on the desk. I rush around to turn on the computer. It's already booted up, and an invoice for a splint is showing as printed on the monitor.

"Brandt," I call down the hall, confused.

I was told he had no idea how to use the accounting software. Any invoices he issues himself are handwritten.

I walk back to his office.

"I do believe you have been holding out on me, Doc," I say as I step in the doorway.

He is sitting behind his desk, and sitting in the chair facing him with a cup of coffee in hand is Miss Elaine.

My heart sinks.

She turns to me with a huge smile on her face, but it instantly drops as she takes in my expression.

"Hi," I whisper.

"Hello, Bellamy. Is everything all right?"

Brandt stands and rounds the desk. "Are you okay?" he asks, his voice laced with concern.

I shake myself out of my moment of upset and force a smile of my own. "I'm good. Just … I'm very sorry I was late," I say as chipper as I can.

"Not a big deal. I was late too," he says, and his eyes are dancing with amusement.

"I'm thrilled to see you, and I am so happy you are here now. I'm jet-lagged, and I can't wait to get upstairs and take a very long nap in my own bed," Elaine says.

"You want me to stay?" I ask.

"Oh, yes—that is, if you don't mind. I'm old, and travel is hard on me. I could use a couple of days to recuperate." She covers her mouth for a long, exaggerated yawn.

Then, she stands and walks around Brandt.

"You two have a productive day," she says before leaving the office and taking the stairs up to their apartment.

"Do you think she knows?" I ask as I watch her until she is out of sight.

"Definitely," he affirms.

"Myer knows too," I tell him.

"Yep, he does."

"Are you okay with that?" I ask without turning to look at him.

"Depends," he says.

"On what?"

"He's not going to come after me with a shotgun or anything, is he?" he asks.

I turn at his question.

He's grinning a sexy grin down at me.

"You know, I'm used to you being so serious all the time. I can't tell when you are teasing or not," I accuse.

He walks to me, brings his hand to the back of my neck, and pulls me in till we are face-to-face. "Of course I'm teasing you. There's no way Myer is going to shoot the only vet in town."

I bow my head, and he presses his lips to my forehead.

"You smell better," I taunt him in return.

He runs his hands up and down my arms. "We have another patient coming in ten minutes. Three more are on the schedule. We'll be done by two o'clock."

"That's an early day," I point out.

"The kitchen goes in today, and I have to get to the house before the contractors leave," he explains.

"How exciting."

"Bellamy, about last night," he begins, and I brace myself.

The bell chimes, signaling our eleven o'clock has arrived.

I groan. I needed that ten minutes.

Relief washes over him, and he releases me. I make my way up to the front desk to greet and check them in.

Saved by the bell.

Thirty-Two

BELLAMY

"HELP, SOMEONE, HELP ME!"

I hear the screamed plea outside the office door and run from around the desk to see Sophie rushing around the front of her truck.

I yell for Brandt and open the door and rush to her aid.

"Sophie, what's wrong?" I ask as I make it to her.

"It's Hawkeye, I was outside bringing groceries in from the truck and he started going nuts and darted out of the door ahead of me. There was a snake at the curb that I hadn't seen and it was raised to strike me but Hawk got to it first and threw himself between it and me. It got him in the leg," she explains breathlessly as she opens the door and tries to lift the dog.

"Don't, let me get him. You don't need to be lifting him," I say as I move her aside and reach in for the lethargic hound.

Just as I make it to the sidewalk, Brandt comes out and, assessing the situation, takes the pup from my arms and Sophie and I follow him inside.

"What got him?" he asks as we make it to the exam room and he sets him on the table.

"A rattlesnake," she answers.

"How long ago?"

"I picked him up and put him straight into the truck and came straight here. I flew so maybe fifteen minutes or so. His face started swelling and he was breathing funny. Panting. He threw up in the truck on the way here too. Please don't let him die," she sobs.

"Bellamy, set up an IV; I need to get fluids started right away. Also, pull a vial of antivenin," he instructs and I hurry to get everything started.

Hawkeye starts seizing on the table and Sophie become hysterical. I go as fast as I can to assist Brandt because I know I need to also help comfort Hawk's very pregnant, distraught mother or we are liable to have two emergencies on our hands if she goes into early labor.

"He's in shock, let's get the fluids in him," Brandt says calmly as he lays Hawk on his side and places a pillow under his hind legs to elevate them. Then he begins to examine his gums and gently tugs his tongue to clear his airway.

I get the bag hung and insert the needle to get the IV going quickly, and then I set the syringes with the medications on the tray by the table. Once I have everything set up for Brandt, I make my way over to Sophie and guide her towards the door of the exam room.

"I don't want to leave him," she cries.

"I know, but I promise he is in good hands. Dr. Haralson will take good care of him. Let's get you some water and call Braxton," I suggest as I carefully tug her into the hallway.

She is shaking and I'm afraid she will fall, so I keep my hands on her back as I lead her to the break room.

Once I have her sitting down, I bring her a bottle of water and then go retrieve her purse from the truck. I grab my cell off the desk on the way out to call Braxton. There is no way I'm letting her drive herself home.

Braxton doesn't answer his phone, so I try Walker's.

"Hello, beautiful, what can I do for you?"

"Is Braxton near you?" I ask as I make it to Sophie's truck. Groceries are slung all over the place. Ice cream is melting, eggs broken and fruit rolling around the backseat and the smell of Hawk's sickness fills the cab.

"Yes, he's up on the tractor, why? Don't tell me she already popped," he says and I can hear his breathing increase as he starts running.

"No, but it's not out of the question. Hawk was bitten protecting

Sophie from a rattlesnake and she drove him to the clinic. Brandt's working on Hawk, but I don't know if he'll make it or not. Sophie is frantic and she needs Braxton in a hurry. Also, her truck needs a cleanup from puppy vomit," I tell him.

"Ten-four," he says and I can make out the muffled conversation as he relays the message to Braxton before coming back on the line.

"We're both on our way."

The line goes dead and I take Sophie's purse to her and let her know her husband is on his way. I make several more trips out to her track to bring the groceries into the clinic and put them in the fridge. By the time I make my last trip, Walker's truck pulls up and Braxton bounds out and runs to the door.

"She's in the break room down the hall on the right," I call to him as he enters.

"Here, let me have those," Walker says as he approaches and relieves me of the bags.

"Thank you," I say as I give him the weight, "I'll lock it up."

"Nah, leave it open and I'll get to cleaning it as soon as we get these in. I'll get as much as I can now and then I'll drive it back to Rustic Peak and give it a good bath and Brax can drive Soph home in my truck."

Sophie is in Braxton's arms weeping when we make it inside. He is rubbing her back and murmuring soothing words into her hair.

"I'll go check in and see what's happening now that you have her," I tell him and he gives me an appreciative nod.

Brandt was able to get Hawkeye settled and the antivenin going in time. After about half an hour, his breathing settled and his heart rate returned to normal.

"I gave him pain meds to help him sleep. I want to keep him here overnight, so I can keep an eye on him. I'm going to give him another round of fluids tonight and I want to see how he does eating in the morning before I release him. The good news is he is going to be okay. The bad news is that he may be blind in that right eye. I won't know for sure until tomorrow when more of the swelling goes down, but I'm fairly certain."

Sophie lets out another agonizing sob.

Braxton tucks her tight into his side.

"It's okay, baby, he's alive and that's all that matters. He still has one eye, and even if he didn't, we'd be his eyes for him if he needed us to be," he tells her and she nods against his shoulder.

She takes a few shaky steps and leans down to rest her face against Hawk's nose.

"I love you, Hawk. So much," she whispers through her tears. He rouses briefly, opens his good eye and licks her nose.

Braxton chuckles softly, then reaches down and lays a hand on top of Hawk's head. He bends down and whispers, "Thank you for protecting our girls while I was at work, buddy."

He straightens and extends his hand to Brandt. "And thank you, Doc. I appreciate you taking care of my family today."

Brandt shakes his hand and smiles.

"Just doing my job."

Braxton inclines his head and leads Sophie out to get her home.

"It's more than a job," I say and he looks back to me.

"To them and to you too. I saw your face when they came in. You were hurting for her but you kept your shit together for them. You're a hero, Doc."

He starts to shake his head and protest.

"You are to me and to those two making their way home right now, you are."

You are pretty special indeed, Brandt Haralson.

Thirty-Three

BRANDT

THE PAST TWO DAYS HAVE BEEN A BLUR. YESTERDAY, I DEALT with contractors. I was impressed enough with the kitchen install that I decided to hire the same crew to finish the work in the master suite. While they took measurements so they could plan the new plumbing route and the new tub and vanity, I started scraping and prepping the outside for painting.

Today, I've been on large-animal house calls all day, only popping into the clinic for supplies and paperwork. Both Bellamy and Mom are in the office, so Bells and I don't really get time to talk.

Now, I'm holding a ladder at Walker's home, so Payne can attach gutters to the three-story roof.

These men know how to work with their hands. Jefferson taught me how to use a table saw to cut lumber for framing. He was patient, and I tried to absorb and retain all the knowledge he was imparting. My dad was a businessman. He taught me the importance of a good education, how to dress for success, and the value of good customer service. However, he didn't show me how to change the oil in my car, wire a new ceiling fan, or how to use a table saw. His hands were soft, and that was okay, but I wish I knew how to build things with my own two hands. I want to learn and am willing to work hard now that I have someone able to teach me.

"I'm coming down, Doc," Payne calls, and I move from my position, holding the ladder steady to the side to let him descend.

"You want to try the next one?" he asks.

"I would, but I have no idea what I'm doing," I admit.

"You just take a pocket of sheet metal screws up and hang this cordless drill on your tool belt. Take a section of the gutter and carry it up. Emmett, Jefferson's best friend and Rustic Peak's caretaker, already measured and divided them, notched the ends, and cut the outlet holes. All you have to do is take the end of your section and line it up with the notched end of the one I hung up. Click it together like this. Then, add a screw with your drill and attach it to the fascia every two feet to secure it. I'll be your anchor, and I'll make sure the ladder stays steady. That's all there is to it."

It sounds like something I could do without fucking it up.

"I'll give it a shot," I agree.

"Let's get it done, then," he says as he removes the tool belt from his waist and hands it off to me.

I go up the first time, and it's awkward to try and hold the gutter in place and screw at the same time, but once I get the hang of the drill and overcome my nerves at letting go of the ladder and extending my reach, it isn't so bad. Payne and I rotate, hanging and holding the rest of the sections until the entire front and right side of the roof is done. Walker and Foster have been tackling the back and left side. They beat us by a good twenty minutes, but we still make good time for being the team with a rookie member.

"Impressive, Doc. You are strong as an ox under those scrubs. Hanging gutters is not for sissies," Payne acknowledges.

"I appreciate your patience with teaching me. I want to learn everything I can." I thank him.

"Stick around. With everyone getting married and having babies, we tend to do a lot of construction nowadays. You'll be a pro in no time."

169

"Thank you, baby," Walker says as he takes the cooler from Elle.

He opens the top and tosses Payne and me a cold beer.

Braxton headed home to his wife an hour ago, and Jefferson and Emmett were right behind him.

"Are we back tomorrow night?" Payne asks.

"Nah, they are calling for storms tomorrow. I'll be at Rustic Peak late, helping to keep an eye on the fences and trees. We'll call it a week. I'm having the sealant put down on the concrete floors Thursday, and that needs time to dry and set," Walker explains.

"That means, you're free Friday, right, babe?" Elle asks.

"Yes, ma'am. I'm all yours."

"Excellent. Bells and I want to go hike at Hickory Nut Gorge," she requests.

"We can do that," he agrees.

"We? I hope you aren't including me in that we. My hiking days are behind me," Payne states.

"Since when? We always have a blast while hiking," Elle asks.

"Since I almost broke my tailbone that last hike," he reminds her.

"That shit was funny as hell," Walker goads.

"It wasn't funny to Dad when I couldn't run a tractor for five weeks because of a chipped coccyx," Payne complains.

"Damn, brother, I didn't know you'd hurt your manhood. Hope it healed okay. Of course, the ladies appreciate a bit of crooked—" Walker interrupts.

"Coccyx, jackass. Not cock. My manhood is just fine, thank you."

"If you say so." Walker shifts his focus to me. "What about you, Doc? Don't leave me hiking with two females alone. If anything happens, I can't carry them both out. I'll have to sacrifice one. You don't want that on your conscience, do you?" he asks.

"Um ..."

"Jeez, will you stop?" Elle hits him in the chest. "If you want a buddy to come out and play with you, ask nicely. Besides, I'm planning to ask Sonia if she and Ricky want to join us when I stop into her mom's shop to check on the poodle skirts for Aunt Doe's party."

"Noooo," Walker whines.

"Yes," she insists.

"Doc, would you enjoy an evening of friendly companionship while engaging in physical activity that is good for your health but potentially dangerous to your coccyx, pretty please?" He bats his eyelashes at me and waits for an answer.

"Sure."

"Yes! Thank you." He does a fist pump.

Payne snickers. "I'm almost compelled to put my manhood in jeopardy to watch Ricky make Walk's head explode."

"It's a strong possibility," Walker agrees.

"If you do anything that causes Sonia any grief, your manhood will be the one in jeopardy," Elle dares.

Walker's hands protectively cover his lap. "You're a mean woman," he accuses.

"I can be, or if you are a nice boy, I can be a very, very good woman." She grins at him coyly.

"See what I'm talking about, Doc? Sexual persuasion. She uses it as a weapon, and I fold like a cheap suit. Every damn time."

Elle winks at me, and Payne bursts into laughter.

Thirty-Four

BELLAMY

ELLE MEETS ME AT THE CLINIC AFTER CLOSING, AND WE WALK down to Sonia's mom, Kathy's shop. She is an excellent seamstress, and she does most of the alterations and embroidery for Poplar Falls. She owned a small fabric and craft store uptown, but this past spring, she rebranded the space and opened a new consignment shop for both vintage clothing and furniture. She gives them a face-lift before adding them to the racks or show floor. The shop is aptly called Plum Nearly New. It's wicked cool. I've found so many unique additions to my wardrobe there.

The shop is closed, so we tap on the window and get Kathy's attention. She comes up and unlocks the dead bolt to let us in.

"Hey, girls," she greets us with a hug. "Sonia will be down in a minute. Come on into the back, and I'll show you what I have done so far."

Sonia and Ricky live in the one-bedroom apartment above her mom's store. Her parents gave it to her to live rent-free as a graduation present. Ricky moved in right before their wedding.

We walk into Kathy's workspace in the back of the store. She has a clothing rack with an array of wool skirts in different colors and sizes. Each one has a hand-stitched poodle in the bottom-right corner.

"These are amazing!" Elle gasps. "Exactly what we wanted."

"Which one is Doreen's?" I ask.

Kathy thumbs through the skirts until she plucks a powder-pink skirt with a black poodle.

"She's going to die," I say in approval.

We have a skirt, bobby socks, and saddle shoes for Doreen, so she can change once we get her to the party and the cat is out of the bag.

"Mine?" I ask.

"Yours isn't ready yet, Bellamy. I had to send off for the turquoise-blue material you'd requested. It should be here the first of next week, and I'll have it done in plenty of time. Same with Sophie's. I failed the first attempt to create a maternity poodle skirt, but I found a pattern online, so I'm giving it another shot."

"Okay, I'll go ahead and pay you for these completed ones and get them out of your way. I'll pay for and pick up the rest next Friday," Elle tells her.

"Sounds good. The skirts are twenty each. That covers all the materials and also a crinoline for each. I'm going to donate my time for Doreen's birthday gift."

"Oh no, we want to pay you. It's a lot of work, and we ordered two dozen of them."

Elle tries to convince her to charge more, but she refuses.

"Nope, I want to do them. Now, scoot," she demands.

Sonia comes in, and we order a pizza from the Pie Junction next door.

We sit on one of the couches and eat and gab as Kathy sews away.

"I'm so happy we are getting to spend a minute together. It feels like we never get to do this anymore," I tell them.

"Same," Sonia agrees.

"Speaking of time together, Bells and I are taking a couple of the fellas and going for a hike on Friday. Are you and Ricky free? We'd love for you guys to join us," Elle invites.

Sonia grimaces. "We can't. It's Ricky's poker night, and we're going to his friend Scott's house," she informs us.

"I thought Saturdays were poker night?" I say.

She nods. "They are."

"So, you have to go to his friend's house and hang out with them two nights in a row every weekend, but he can't come to spend one afternoon with us?" I ask her to clarify.

"I know. It's just … he gets the impression that my guy friends don't like him, and he says he doesn't want to spend an evening playing pretend just to make me happy."

"Do you like all his friends?" Elle asks.

She shrugs. "They're okay. Of course, they aren't you guys, but I can enjoy myself with the wives while the husbands play, I guess."

"You want to come with us? Let him go to his poker game, and you come out and then spend the night with us. We'll have a slumber party, for old times' sake," Elle pushes.

"I can't. I like taking Ricky and being able to drive him home. They get so sloshed when they play, and I stay sober because I like to sleep in my big bed, not in the tiny twin-size guest beds they have."

"All right," Elle huffs.

"He's my husband," Sonia murmurs.

Elle presses her lips together.

"I know. And we don't want to steal you guys' time together with his people. We just miss you. That's all." I pout.

"We'll figure something out so that we can see each other more," Sonia promises.

Elle sticks out her pinkie finger, and Sonia wraps her own around it.

"Pinkie swear. Now, you're legally required to make it happen."

"Now, let's talk about Bellamy and Brandt Haralson." Elle turns the conversation onto me.

"What do you want to know?"

"Progress report," Elle says.

I blow out a breath. I don't really want to discuss Brandt and me at the moment because I have no idea what to report, but the three of us tell each other everything. We have no secrets. So, I tell them all that has transpired up to this point.

They both sit there with their mouths agape.

"Wow, in the river and the shower?" Sonia asks.

"And the bathroom counter?" Elle adds.

"Yep," I confirm.

"Ricky and I have only had sex in a bed or on a couch," Sonia complains.

"Walker and I like to have sex outdoors too," Elle confesses.

"Outdoors?" Sonia shrieks.

"Yep, on hikes, on the hood of the truck in parking lots, and in the fishing boat." She ticks off each place on her fingers.

"The fishing boat that he took Beau and me out on?" I ask in disbelief.

She nods.

"How? That thing is tiny," I ask, fascinated.

"I straddle him while he fishes. The last time, I climaxed as he reeled in our dinner."

"No way. You just made that up," Sonia accuses.

"Cross my heart. It was just last weekend."

"He's changed you. You went from my sweet, shy friend to a sexual deviant," Sonia tells her.

"Wicked—that's what he makes me feel. And that's because I feel safe enough to be myself with him. Just him. It's everything."

A mournful expression casts over Sonia.

"I thought we were talking about Bells's sexcapades. Stop deflecting and spill." Elle brings the attention back to me.

"Not much else to tell. That's all the progress that I have to report."

"So, are you a couple now?" Sonia asks, clearly back in the game.

"I don't know. I don't think so though. He doesn't seem ready for anything with a label."

"You came for him three times the other night, and Elle didn't even get to second base when they dated. I'd say he flew right past the casual stage with you."

"Maybe I seduced him. Not intentionally, but I did strip down and jump in the river," I admit.

"You devil temptress," Elle teases.

"I was," I insist.

"If he didn't want you, he wouldn't have chased you into the water. He could have easily turned around and walked back to the house. Men aren't as helpless against us as they let on. They are helpless only if they want you bad enough," Sonia declares.

"She's right. I can get Walker to agree to anything if I attack him but only because he likes it. We know there used to be a gaggle of women willing to do whatever he wanted to get more from him, and he didn't fall for their antics. He ignored them. He doesn't ignore me because he doesn't want to. Sometimes, I think he says no to stuff he wants to say yes to just so I will try to change his mind."

We all giggle.

"So, you guys think I should do, what?" I ask because I need some advice.

"Tell him what you want," Elle suggests.

I wrinkle my nose at the idea.

"Or just keep showing up and see if he makes the next move," Sonia counters.

I like that idea much better.

Chicken.

Thirty-Five

BRANDT

"SLOW DOWN, WOMAN. THIS ISN'T A RACE," WALKER CALLS ahead to Elle and Bellamy.

The two have been happily gabbing and trotting carefree up the trail. The very long, steep trail. Walker and I, on the other hand, have had to take several rest stops and water breaks while they stand and impatiently wait for us.

"This is why you don't date younger girls. At first, it's all thrilling and hot, and then at some point, you realize the woman is trying to kill you," Walker mutters.

"Oh, quit whining, old, fat guy, and keep up," she calls back to him.

"She knows being mean and bossy turns me on. She's playing me like a fiddle," he gripes.

The sound of their giggles drifts back to us.

Walker whistles low and elbows my side.

"Would you look at that? Have you ever seen anything more beautiful?" he asks, awe clear in his voice.

I look at the twin mountain peaks in the distance with clouds dancing around them. "Spectacular."

"Fucking incredible. And I'm not talking about the view," he clarifies.

He is not wrong. The two friends tangled together ahead of us are exquisite.

"We are some lucky SOBs, Doc," he states.

The four of us run into a couple of male hikers who are making their way back out of the trail, and as they pass Elle and Bellamy, who are still a considerable distance ahead of us, they stop and turn to watch our girls as they walk on, oblivious to the attention.

Our girls?

"Tongues back in, boys. They would chew you up and spit you out. You don't need that kind of trouble in your life. Go hump a cheerleader or something," Walker says as we pass the drooling duo.

Then, we watch as the girls hook arms and chatter away as they keep walking, full steam ahead.

Two hours later, we reach the apex of the grueling trek. Bellamy and Elle are at the top when we crest the edge. They are standing to the side, framed by a breathtaking view, and Bellamy has Elle riding piggyback. She is holding one of Elle's legs clamped around her with one hand, and she has her cell phone extended in the other. The two of them are making silly faces into the camera and snapping selfies. Elle starts slipping down Bellamy's back, and her running shorts start to slide with her. Bellamy lets out a yelp and drops Elle and her phone, and they both tumble to the ground in a heap of female limbs. They are squealing and laughing and rolling in the grass.

"What did you two get into while we were back there?" Walker asks as we stand over them.

They stop wiggling and look up at us. Tears leaking down their cheeks from laughing.

Walker leans down and extends both arms to them. They each grasp a hand, and he pulls them to their feet.

"Can't take you two anywhere."

We all sit on a log that faces out to the view until the sun starts to set. Elle ends up on the grass in front of Walker, and he wraps her in his arms to shield her from the cold wind that is kicking up around us.

"Are you cold?" I ask Bellamy, and she tells me she's fine.

I see the gooseflesh down her exposed arms and know that she's lying.

I pull off my long-sleeved moisture-wicking shirt and pull it over her head. She bites her lip and then raises her arms, so I can slip it on her.

"Thank you," she whispers.

I thread my fingers into her hair and tug the band loose. Her gorgeous hair falls down her back and around her face.

"There, that will keep the wind off your neck," I say in explanation. But the truth is, I love her hair. I like it down and wild.

Her expectant eyes look up into mine, and I bring my hand to the side of her face, rubbing my thumb over her cheek. Her lips part slightly at my touch, and I can feel her pulse quicken at her throat. My touch does that. My gaze drops to her mouth, and a need to taste her again rages under my skin. I lean in and run my nose to hers, and just as my mouth finds hers, a bolt of lightning flashes in the distance followed by a loud, thunderous boom that shakes the ground beneath us. I jerk my head to look out at the horizon.

"Shit, how close do you think that is?" Walker asks as he looks to me over Elle's shoulder.

"About three, maybe four miles. We'd better head back," I tell him.

He stands and pulls Elle to her feet. I help Bellamy up and guide her in front of me. We move quickly, but this time, Walker and I stay close to them. Before we can make it off the trail, the lightning is on us, and we can see it striking ground around us. I shield Bellamy with my body, and she is trembling.

"You okay?" I ask as we speed up, Walker and Elle staying in step with us.

"I don't like lightning," she divulges, and I can tell she is closing her eyes and not watching where she's going.

Fat, cold raindrops start to fall heavily around us. Bellamy stumbles over her feet, and I grasp her shoulder and keep her upright. She is terrified. I halt her and turn her into me.

"Hop up," I tell her.

She looks at me, and I open my arms in invitation. She jumps up, and I hoist her up and feed my arms around her hips. She wraps her legs around me tightly. She buries her face into my neck, and I take off sprinting toward the opening to the trail that leads out to the parking area.

By the time we make it to Walker's truck, the rain is pounding down on us in sheets. I hear the truck beep, and the locks disengage just as Walker skids up to us with Elle in his arms. He drops her on her feet, and I set Bellamy on hers. They cling to each other as I move to pull open the door for them as Walker hops in and gets the truck started. I guide them both into the backseat, and I run around the truck to get in the passenger seat.

There is no way Walker can see to head home. The rain is too heavy. I look back, and the girls are huddled and shivering. I turn the heat on full blast, and I aim the vents toward them.

Walker looks at me. "That came out of nowhere. They weren't calling for bad weather tonight. It was supposed to start tomorrow evening."

"It was moving fast. It'll blow over soon," I assume.

Ten minutes later, the rain stops, and the sky clears.

I open the door and walk back to Elle's door.

"Switch with me, sweetheart," I tell her, and I help her out and into the front with Walker.

She scoots across the bench seat to him, and he wraps her in his arm before he pulls out of the parking lot.

I pull Bellamy's back into me, and I wrap both arms around her to warm her.

"Better?" I ask in her ear.

"I want doughnuts."

That's her answer, and it tells me all I need to know. She's good. And I'm getting her doughnuts.

I ask Walker if he knows of any doughnut shops open anywhere. He drives us all the way to Aurora to Winchell's Doughnut House, which is open twenty-four seven. The girls don't want to go inside because they are soaking wet, so I go in and buy two-dozen assorted doughnuts and four cups of coffee.

When we make it back to Poplar Falls, Walker drives us to town and drops us at my SUV. Bellamy climbs in with her Winchell's box.

I start the ignition and get the heat going. Then, I head toward her house. When we make it to Stoney Ridge, she doesn't move to get out. She just waits for me to do or say something. I reach and take the box from her, and I set it on the dash. Then, I chuckle, and she turns to me in surprise.

I wipe the powdered sugar from the corner of her mouth with my thumb, and then I bring it to my mouth and suck it off.

Her eyes widen as she watches me. Then, she darts up and wraps her arms around my neck. I pull her in close, and my mouth finds hers. Her kiss is urgent and needy as the stress exits her body, and desire takes its place. I know I can't satisfy her in my truck in front of her parents' home. I want to. I want to watch her splinter as I give her what she needs. Instead, I kiss her hard. Then, I pull away and kiss her nose and her eyes and her forehead as I caress her back.

She sighs as she leans back and opens her eyes. "I'm sorry about the freak-out. I don't know where it comes from, but lightning is one thing I don't do. Give me five feet of snow any day over a heat-seeking, cracking electrical current."

"Being afraid is nothing to be sorry about. We all have our triggers. I bet studying environmental science contributed to this fear."

"Yep. You should have seen the videos they showed us. Lightning striking a fuel hauler while they were driving down the road or entering someone's bay windows and flowing through the oven before zapping them as they removed a pan. It also causes forest fires that spread beyond control. It's awful. Plus, I was traumatized by a fire lightning caused at my grandparents' when I was a little girl."

She starts to explain when the porch light clicks on. I know that Winston was waiting for her, and he saw the minute we pulled in. He has been giving us a little more alone time each time I drop her off.

"I guess that's my cue." She stops her story short.

I jump out to open her door, and I grab the box before leading her to the front door. Winston raises an eyebrow at her drowned appearance.

"The bottom fell out on us, Poppy," she says.

"I can see that."

"I'm going to take a shower." She turns to me. "Thank you, Doc."

"Sweet dreams, sweetheart," I tell her before she disappears.

The door shuts behind her, and Winston turns back to me.

"Appreciate you getting her home safe again, Brandt."

I don't answer. I just hand him the box.

He reads the name on the top, and he grins hugely.

"Good man, Brandt," he says sincerely. "You're a good man."

Thirty-Six

BELLAMY

I SPEND MOST OF SATURDAY IN BED WITH A COLD. MOMMA MADE ME homemade chicken soup and kept bringing me ginger ale and medication. I know I'm technically an adult, but when I don't feel well, all I want is my momma. Her presence alone makes me feel better.

I finally start to feel human again at around six o'clock. In my pajamas, I get up and make my way to the couch with a fuzzy blanket.

Momma and Pop rode over to Myer's to see Faith, and the house is too quiet. I click on the television and surf until I find the ID channel. My roomie and I got addicted to true-crime stories when I was in Chicago. I find something comforting about watching murder. Nope, doesn't make any sense, but it's true.

I snuggle in and get lost in a show about a football player who killed his best friend for vague reasons.

The phone rings, and I answer.

"Hey, Bellamy. I just wanted to call and check on you. Your mom said you were sick," Dallas says.

I can hear Pop talking gibberish to Faith in the background.

"I'm a little better. Just taking it easy."

"I have some leftover chicken potpie from dinner, if you want me to wrap it up for you."

Dallas and her mom make the best chicken potpie in the world. She knows it's my favorite.

"Yes, please," I answer when thunder rolls outside. "Dang it. It's thundering here," I say.

"This weather has been nuts. The storms cause Cowboy to have a panic attack. Good thing Brandt is here to see it this time."

"Brandt is there?"

"Yeah, apparently, he didn't make it to Cowboy's appointment on Monday, so he offered to come and give him his shots today," she explains.

"Right. That's thoughtful."

Thunder rumbles again, and the sky lights up outside.

"So, I'll throw in some muffins too, and …" Dallas keeps talking, but I don't hear anything else.

There is a strange glow in the front yard, so I walk to the door with the phone still to my ear.

The barn. The barn is on fire. No.

"The barn. Shit, Dallas, the horses," I cry over her.

"What?"

"The barn is on fire. I have to go." The last thing I hear is Dallas screaming for Myer. I drop the phone and take off running toward the barn.

The fire is spreading rapidly, and I can hear the fearful cries of the horses as I approach. Pop and Foster stalled them because the storms were coming.

I get to the door, and it's warm to the touch. I wrap my hand in my pajama top and reach for the handle. I can feel the metal burning my hand through the fabric.

I race into the engulfed barn without thought. I grab a saddle blanket from a hook near the door and wrap it around me as I run to the stalls. I can hear the horses' panicked whinnies, and I make my way to the last door and fling it open first. The mare bucks up on her hind legs in fear, and I grab her rein and tug. She finally comes out of the stall. I slap her rear, and she bolts for the door. I go to the next door, fling it open, and repeat. And then the next.

The flames are dancing higher, and wood is falling from the roof. I try to hold my breath as long as I can, but my body involuntarily inhales on one of my cries, and my lungs fill with smoke. I make it to the final door as Pop, Myer, Truett, and Brandt come skidding into the blazing building, screaming my name. Pop spots me and comes running.

"Ali!" I yell.

"We'll get him," he promises as he wraps his arm around my shoulders and leads me out into the fresh air. The boys search the barn and free the last of the horses safely from their stall. I thankfully see the colt stagger out ahead of his mother.

Once we clear the threshold, I stumble and fall to my backside in the gravel, sputtering and coughing. Relieved to know Ali made it out.

Momma comes running to my side.

"Oh, Bellamy, are you okay, sweetheart?" she asks, panicked.

I just nod as tears flood my vision to soothe my stinging eyes.

Sirens fill the air around us as two fire trucks come barreling through the gate.

"Oh, thank goodness," Momma mutters.

"You got her?" Pop asks, and she nods to him.

He takes off jogging to meet the firemen.

Myer, Brandt, and Truett emerge from the back of the barn, and Brandt heads straight for me. I sit up and take the water bottle Momma offers.

His wild eyes comb the length of me from head to toe.

Then, he begins to pace. Running his hands through his hair over and over.

"Brandt," I call to him, my voice hoarse.

He stops and looks at me. "You ran into a burning building," he says angrily.

"I-I had to get the horses out. They were trapped in there," I begin to explain.

"You saw the barn was on fire, and you ran to it and went in. Into a fire."

"Brandt, son," Pop calls to him.

"You could have died, Bellamy," he continues.

"I didn't. I'm right here," I remind him.

"You could have been killed. You ran into a fucking building that was on fire," he roars.

I look up to Momma for help.

"Brandt, come here." She pats the ground between us.

He looks from the spot to her and then to me.

"I have to go," he mutters, more to himself than to us.

"Okay," I say.

He looks at me one last time, and then he stomps off to the driveway behind the fire trucks.

Tears prick my eyes … *or is it rain?*

The sky opens up, and the rain starts to pour. I just sit there and let it soak me again as I watch the firemen fight to put out the flames. They cheer when the rain shows up, aiding their efforts.

Thirty-Seven

BRANDT

I PULL INTO THE HOUSE. I'M TOO WORKED UP TO GO HOME TO THE apartment. I slam the truck door and walk to the entrance. The rain is beating down on me.

I fumble with my keys in the dark until I find the one I'm searching for, and I let myself in. I click on the light and look around. So much progress has been made. New windows were cut and installed this week. Bellamy was right; the natural light makes all the difference. The kitchen is modern and functional yet oddly still fits with the Colonial feel of the two-hundred-fifty-year-old home. It's perfect on the surface, but inside, it's empty. Just like me.

Seeing Bellamy running from the burning barn and collapsing on the ground shook me in a way I hadn't thought was possible anymore. The feeling of absolute uselessness suffocated me as I hid in my SUV and watched as the ambulance pulled off with her and her mother inside.

Fuck. How did I get here again?

I kick off my shoes, and I make my way upstairs. I empty my pockets, and then I pull my soggy clothes off and drop them on the tiled floor of the bathroom. I turn back, and I practically face-plant on the bed, naked.

I lie there a long while and listen to the rain against the roof. Then, I climb under the covers and fall asleep.

I walk up on the scene once again. The same one that plays through my mind most nights. I stand helplessly as I watch Annie pulling on her coat as she leaves the restaurant in a huff and starts to walk out to the parking lot. My attention snaps to the dumpster on the left, and I brace for what is coming next as a shadowy figure huddles close to it, watching her as she opens her purse and starts fishing for her keys.

Look up, Annie. Look at your surroundings.

She finds the keys and clicks the button to unlock the car doors.

No, don't do that. Don't unlock them until you are there.

She swipes at the angry tears falling from her lashes.

I look at her beautiful, sad face one last time before it happens.

The dark figure stands and runs to the passenger side of her car. She is distracted by her phone—by my text messages—and she doesn't see him.

Look up, Annie, please.

The man comes around the car, and he dives for her. He latches on to her purse handle that is on her shoulder and yanks.

Don't fight him. Let him take it. Let him have whatever he wants. None of it means anything.

She grabs for the purse and starts to struggle with him. She tugs the strap back on to her shoulder, and it slips from his hand. She backs away from him. A look of pure terror on her face.

Scream, Annie. Scream and cause a scene, anything to get attention, and he'll flee.

She does none of that. She just stares at him in shock.

He runs for her as he pulls a switchblade from the pocket of his dirty coat, and he stabs her in the stomach. She goes down to a knee. Still holding on to the purse. He pulls the knife back and wildly slashes in the air.

That's when I arrive, and I watch as he slits my Annie's throat from ear to ear. She lets go, and her hands go up to hold the slash. He yanks the purse free of her and takes off behind the restaurant.

I race to her, screaming for help and for someone to call 911. When I make it to her, I pull her head and shoulders into my lap while pleading with her not to leave me. I lean down to kiss her head, and suddenly, it's not Annie. It's not her throat slit from ear to ear.

It's Bellamy.

Her eyes staring at me as she gurgles blood.

Dying in my arms.

I wake with a start, covered in sweat with my heart pounding. Victim to a new nightmare.

Thirty-Eight

BELLAMY

THE FIREMAN INSISTS I GO TO THE EMERGENCY ROOM TO BE checked out. When I arrive, my oxygen levels are low, and my lungs and throat are irritated due to the heat and smoke I have inhaled. I also suffer from a few small burns to my forearms, palms, and neck.

I'm admitted, and they give me oxygen and nebulizer treatments to help my lungs recover.

My voice is gone. Just gone.

I panic when I wake up and can't talk because I think it's permanent. I fight the nurses and Momma, who is sleeping at the hospital with me. Refusing to leave her daughter alone. I rip out my IV and start bleeding everywhere, so once they get me to settle down; they make the decision to medicate me more heavily to keep me calm and pain-free while I heal.

Everyone in Poplar Falls comes through my room for the next two days. And I do mean everyone, except for Brandt. Even Miss Elaine stops in. Pop Lancaster and Jefferson just happen to be dropping off flowers when she arrives. Pop sits down beside her, and they strike up a conversation. One that lasts a couple of hours. Long after Jefferson has left. I kind of feel like a voyeur as they chat, and I doze on and off.

Brandt sends his regards through his mother as well as a lovely bouquet of white tulips, however he is extremely busy and can't make it by.

On day two, a ridiculously huge bouquet of silver roses—my favorite—are delivered, and I cry, thinking they must be from Brandt as well, but it turns out, they are from Derrick. I have had him blocked for over a month, but apparently, he has continued to call my parents' house. Momma has been effectively blowing him off for weeks, per my request, but Pop answered while we were both at the hospital and told him everything.

"I don't want them. Give them to my nurse," I tell the delivery lady when I read the card.

I still can't believe Brandt hasn't come to see me. I miss him. I've called his cell a couple of times, but it goes straight to voice mail, and I don't leave a message.

I figure I'm just overreacting. He knows I'm good. He was there that night, and it obviously freaked him out. It's only been a few days.

By the time they release me, I'm so over the hospital. I'm fine. I want to go home, and I make that perfectly clear to anyone within earshot.

I think they finally cut me loose just so they don't have to hear it any longer.

Lightning was determined to be the cause of the barn fire. It had somehow struck into a crack on the roof or come through the tiny window to the loft and ignited the bales of hay stored in there.

Damn lightning.

I won't be scared of it any longer though. I went toe to toe with its wrath and defeated it.

Pop and Myer salvaged what they could from the fire, and they already have the framing done for the new and improved barn.

Jefferson Lancaster has offered to temporarily store anything we need and help tend to our horses until we can raise our new barn.

Once I'm home, I take it easy for another week as Momma fusses over me nonstop.

Still no word from Brandt.

I finally leave the house to go to Sophie's for a party-planning meeting.

The party is happening this weekend, and every detail needs to be finalized.

When I get back home, Momma informs me I have a message on the answering machine. My heart skips at the hope that it's Brandt, but why would he call the house and not my cell?

I press play, and it's Dr. Singh's office from the Denver Zoo, asking me to call as soon as possible.

I jot the number down and head to my room.

To my surprise, when I return the call, I'm patched through to Dr. Singh himself.

"Bellamy, I'm so glad you got back to me. I realize this is short notice, and that's why I wanted to reach out to you personally. The animal nutritionist position has just opened back up, and we'd like to offer it to you, if you are still available."

I don't reply as I roll this information over in my mind.

"I was told you'd chosen someone else," I say in answer.

"The board did, yes. They decided to go with a grad student, but the applicant reached out to us a couple of days ago and rescinded his acceptance. You were always my first choice, so I called you as soon as I was notified. I'd love to have you on my staff."

This is amazing. It's what I've wanted all along. So, why do I feel like crying?

"Bellamy? Are you still there?"

"Yes, I'm sorry. When would you need me in Denver?" I ask.

"I had hoped to have someone here by the end of August, but since that is days away, I'm hoping you can start by mid-September. Can you have your affairs in order and get moved by then?" he asks.

Yes! I scream at myself internally to respond.

"Do you need an answer right this minute? Because I'd like to talk to my family first, if that's okay," I ask instead.

"Of course. I know I sprang this on you. I'll have my secretary email you over the job offer with all the specifics. Take the weekend to look over the paperwork and let me know your decision by Monday."

"I'll do that. And, Dr. Singh? Thank you for believing in me," I say before I hang up.

This is unexpected. I should be elated, but I'm not.

I send Elle a text, telling her I need a bestie night with her and Sonia, stat.

Thirty-Nine

BELLAMY

ELLE AND SONIA ARE AT MY DOORSTEP WITHIN THE HOUR.
I tell them about Brandt avoiding me and about my phone
call with Dr. Singh.

After a couple of mugs of cocoa with extra marshmallows, we decide that I should talk to Brandt and find out why he suddenly went radio silent before I make any decision regarding Denver.

"Tackle one issue at a time. Then, you'll have all the facts before you make any life-altering plans. Either way, you know we have your back," Sonia encourages.

"Do you want me to call Brandt? He might confide in me," Elle asks.

"No, I appreciate the offer, but I'm a big girl, and I can talk to him myself. It's not like we had any commitment to each other or anything. We were growing closer. At least, I thought we were. I just don't know what happened for him to do a one-eighty like that, and to be honest, I didn't realize how I'd been growing attached to him until he disappeared from my life," I tell them.

"Whatever it is, I think he'll come around. You know I adore him, but he was so closed off. He is different with you. It's like you opened a jar that was shut too tightly. We all tried to open it, but all we could do was wiggle it loose a little. You came along and twisted it right off."

"Well, I think someone has screwed it back on," I tell her.

"Just give him a chance to explain," she says

Elle makes me reach out to him before they leave.

I call his phone and leave him a message. "Hi, it's Bellamy. I know you're busy, but I really would like to see you. Have a conversation about us at least. You know, like grown-ups or something. Please call or text me when you get this."

He doesn't get back to me until hours later, and when he does, it's a text.

I'll be escorting Mom to the party tomorrow night. Are you available afterward? We could come back to the clinic and chat.

Back to the clinic and chat?

I guess if that is the best I'm going to get, I'll take it, so I'll get the chance to tell him to his face exactly what a jerk he is.

Works for me.

I send the reply and throw my phone on the nightstand.

Men think we are the frustrating ones. At this point, I'm thinking a nunnery is a good career choice.

"Where are you?" Elle asks over the line as I make my way to Rustic Peak the next day.

"I'm about a half-mile away," I tell her.

"Hurry, please. Aunt Doe is a wreck. I think she is cracking under the pressure," she whispers into the phone.

"I'll be there in five."

"Okay, bye."

The line goes dead, and I press the gas and rush to Elle's aid.

I pull up to the house ten minutes later and hurry inside.

"Are you two ready to go?" I call as I walk through to the kitchen.

Aunt Doreen is fluttering about. She is taking her responsibility for getting Elle to her "surprise" engagement party very seriously.

"Where's Elle?" I ask as I walk over and pluck a muffin from the basket on the counter.

"She's still getting ready. She came out here in jeans and a T-shirt. I had to make up something on the spot to get her to change clothes because I know she'll want to look nice in the pictures from her party," she rattles off nervously.

"What did you tell her?" I ask around a mouthful of blueberry crumble.

"I told her I wanted us all to get fancied up for dinner. Oh, now, I have to go find something fancified to put on too. I don't have anything fancy. Why did I say that? It doesn't even make sense. This is why I don't lie. I'm so bad at it. You girls never should have trusted me to be the one to get her there. Do you think she's suspicious?"

She is a flustered mess.

"You always look nice, Aunt Doe. I think what you are wearing is fine, and I doubt she suspects a thing," I reassure her.

She looks down at her light-purple blouse that has tiny yellow flowers all over it and her tan dress pants, and she frowns. "But I wear this all the time. Do you think I should change, so she buys it?"

I look up at her. "No?" It comes out as a question instead of an answer.

"You're right. I should change. I'll put on my chocolate-brown blouse, switch to my nice dress shoes, and put on my pearls. Maybe add on some blush," she says more to herself than me as she hurries out of the kitchen.

Five minutes later, and Elle walks in, wearing a pink maxi dress with drop shoulders, and her makeup is flawless.

I whistle.

"She made me change clothes and do my face," she whispers and rolls her eyes. Then, she looks around. "Where did she go?"

"She's upstairs, putting on a fancier blouse and shoes, so you don't catch on to her tricks," I say on a grin.

She smiles. "She's really falling for it."

"Yep. Hook, line, and sinker. She's a nervous wreck," I agree.

I look down at my phone.

"We have to get her out of here, so Jefferson, Emmett, and Pop can get ready and beat us there," I tell her.

"I know. How was I supposed to guess she'd make me change? It threw us behind."

We hear footfalls coming down the stairs in the living room and hurry to meet her.

I elbow Elle, and she clears her throat.

"Don't you look nice?" she praises her aunt as she makes it to the landing.

"You think so?"

"Yes, ma'am, and Bells just called her momma to tell her to put on a nice blouse and shoes too. Look at us, getting all dressed up for girls' evening out. How fun!" Elle says excitedly as she claps her hands.

"Too much," I say under my breath on a fake cough.

"Um, let's get this show on the road. I'm starving." Elle hurries us out the door.

"I'll drive," I offer, and we head over to my Mustang and climb in.

We get about twenty minutes up the road when Doreen's phone chimes with a text. I watch in the mirror as she checks it and bites her lip.

"Bellamy, I forgot something back at the house. Can we run back real quick?"

I look over at Elle in confusion, and she gives me a slight shrug.

"Don't we have reservations?" I ask her.

"Yes, but I'll let them know we are running a tad late. I have a little something for your mother I meant to bring with us, and absent-minded me forgot it," she says.

"Okay." I give in and turn around, heading back for Rustic Peak.

We pass by Jefferson's truck.

"Hey, isn't that Uncle Jefferson?" Elle asks. "I wonder where he and Emmett could be headed to."

"Oh, who knows? They probably didn't want to eat what Ria made for dinner," Doreen says on a nervous laugh.

Like that's a plausible explanation.

Once we pull in, Doreen opens her door.

"I'll be back in a jiffy," she says before attempting to climb out. "Oh, fiddle. I don't know how you girls get in and out of these ole, low cars," she mutters as she heaves herself out of the Mustang.

Once she is inside, Elle pulls her phone out and starts to type. Then, she snickers.

"Dottie was running late with the cake, so they texted Aunt Doreen to tell her to stall," she explains.

"Oh my, she is sweating like a groom the night before the wedding. The woman is going to have a heart attack before we even make it to her party. And nice move, pointing out Jefferson's truck. She went completely white."

Elle giggles. "I know. I'm having so much fun with this."

The door opens, and Doreen comes out, carrying a wrapped box. Who knows what she found to wrap up at the last minute?

Once she settles back in, we are off again.

We swing by Stoney Ridge and pick up my momma, and then we finally make it to the party venue. We pile out of the car, and Doreen grabs her wrapped gift and falls into line behind us.

As we approach the front of the building, Elle slows and tries her best to get her aunt to move out in front of her, so she can walk through the door first, but Doreen keeps slowing down even further. It's comical. At this rate, it's going to take us another thirty minutes just to make it in from the car to the door.

Elle finally gives up and trots up the steps with Momma, Doreen, and me in tow.

"Are you sure we're at the right place, Aunt Doreen? It looks awfully dark in there," Elle asks, and I try not to laugh.

Doreen turns her panicked eyes to me. "I'm positive. It must just be dark curtains," she mumbles, and I can see the beads of nervous sweat at her brow.

I give her a reassuring wink, and as soon as Elle reaches for the door, I hear the bubble of excitement escape Doreen's throat as she braces for everyone to jump out and yell, *Surprise*, at Elle.

Instead, the room stays dark and quiet.

"Hello?" Elle says, walking deeper inside. "No one is here," she calls back over her shoulder.

Doreen walks up, confused, and peers into the door.

"What's … hello!" she says, and her voice cracks.

Two seconds later, the lights flicker on.

Elle turns quickly on her heels among everyone, and we all shout, "Gotcha, Doe!"

She stumbles back a step into me, and I whisper, "Happy birthday, Aunt Doreen."

She looks at me in shock and then takes everyone in. The girls are all dressed in poodle skirts and bobby socks, and the guys are in everything from letterman sweaters to leather jackets and white tees. The jukebox in the corner comes to life and starts to play an Elvis Presley song as Emmett comes out, dressed in a greaser outfit with his hair slicked back.

He takes her hand. "Welcome to your sock hop, sweetheart," he says on a grin.

Then, he leads her inside.

Forty

BELLAMY

DOREEN IS IN TEARS THE ENTIRE TIME WE ARE IN THE restroom, getting into our outfits.

"You had no clue?" Elle asks as she pulls the crinoline up under her skirt.

"No! I thought I was distracting you—and doing a horrible job of it." She sniffles.

"I can't believe we were able to get one over on you. You're the most observant, all-knowing person I know," I tell her.

"You guys came up with the perfect ruse."

"That was all Bellamy," Elle admits.

"Hey, did anyone see Sonia out there?" I ask as I swipe on some red lipstick.

"Yes, I saw her and Ricky at a table up front. She said she'd be in here in a minute, and she wants you and me to wait for her," Elle says.

"Well, girls, how do I look?" Doreen turns in front of the full-length mirror.

Her short hair is spiked up a little, and she has a sheer handkerchief at her neck tied into a bow. Her short-sleeved cream sweater with a cursive *L, for Lancaster,* embroidered across the left breast, is tucked into her poodle skirt, and she has on cream socks and a pair of black-and-white saddle shoes.

"Like a classic fox," I coo.

"Oh," she says and waves away my comment as she blushes.

"Go on, birthday girl. Go grab your man and get him to twirl you around the dance floor," Elle encourages.

She wipes under her eyes one more time before she takes off.

We are just sliding on our shoes when Sonia comes in with a large black bag.

"I have gifts," she squeals.

She sets the bag at our feet and starts to pull the contents out.

There are three shiny pink jackets with *Pink Ladies* on the back.

"No, you didn't," I say as I take one.

"I sure did."

Grease and *Grease 2* are our all-time favorites. We have watched them over and over since we were young. I grew up wanting to be Stephanie Zinone.

"These are the most!" Elle says in her best Patty Simcox voice.

We all slip into the jackets and a pair of black Wayfarer sunglasses, and then we prance out together.

Walker starts to whistle as we all turn and pose.

Sophie snaps a hundred pictures, and then we start to mingle. Brandt and his mom are seated with Pop Lancaster, Ria, Jefferson, and his wife, Madeline. He avoids my eyes as I stop by to say hello to the table.

"You look adorable, Bellamy," Miss Elaine gushes.

"Thank you. You look pretty snazzy yourself."

She is dressed in a house dress and pearls à la Lucy Ricardo. Brandt is in jeans, and a white tee with a box rolled up in the sleeve. His hair is mussed, and he looks like a greaser who just had a woman pressed against a muscle car with her hands pulling at it.

A cry sails through the air, and my eyes follow it. Myer and Dallas are sitting at a table with Beau. Faith is in Dallas's arms, and she is bouncing her as she tries to carry on a conversation with Faye, her old boss at the diner.

"Excuse me, but I think my niece is putting out the *Auntie, come rescue me* distress call," I say before beelining to my sister-in-law and relieving her of the baby.

Elle and Sonia join me in fawning all over her in her tiny onesie with a poodle on the left corner and a pink tutu.

We are all on the floor, dancing Faith around, when Ricky comes and tugs Sonia to the side.

"Scott texted, and everyone is there. Can we head over now?"

"What?" Sonia asks, confused.

"It's Saturday. I told them we'd be over after we popped in here for a few minutes," he says like she should have known.

"We're not leaving, Ricky. I did a lot of prepping and helped plan this party for Doreen. A woman who practically helped raise me. I want to stay."

He shrugs. "Suit yourself. Find a way home. I figure the game will run late tonight," he says before walking away.

Sonia follows him. I hand the baby off to my mom, and Elle and I go with her.

"Are you kidding me right now?" she shouts after him once we are in the hallway.

He turns. "Do I look like I'm kidding?"

"I spend every Friday and Saturday night doing what you want to do, with the people you want to do it with. I barely get to see my own friends anymore. I ask for you to come with me this one time, and you are bailing to go drink beer and play cards at your friend's smoky trailer, like we do every other freaking weekend?"

"Yeah. I came here and made an appearance for you, and now, I'm bored."

"Bored? There is food and a dance floor and an open bar, for goodness' sake," she screams at him.

"I ate. I had a whiskey. I don't like to dance. You know this."

"You are the worst. Do you know that? I keep making excuses for you and doing everything I can to keep you happy, and you do absolutely nothing to make sure I am. You make no effort with my friends. You make no effort for me. I thought if I just hung in there and gave us time, then things would get better, but you don't want better.

You're completely content with the way things are. Content with your wife crying herself to sleep most nights. Content with embarrassing me in front of the whole town."

He just rolls his eyes at her words.

"Do you even love me anymore, Ricky? Did you ever love me?"

"Of course I love you. But that doesn't mean I have to love these people. I didn't marry them. I married you."

"Yes, you kind of did. Because they are part of me. A big part, and if you hate them, then you hate a big part of me. That might be fine for you, but that's not the life I want."

His phone chimes, and he looks down at it.

"We'll talk about this later. I've got to go," he says before walking out the door.

"Are you fucking kidding me?" I say to Elle as we watch Sonia run to the restroom in tears.

I should go after her, but my legs carry me to the exit, and I chase after her good-for-nothing husband.

"I cannot believe you," I screech as I follow Ricky out into the parking lot.

He stops and turns to face me as Elle makes it to my back.

"Don't you think you need to stay and work things out with your wife?" I ask.

"Why don't you go and soothe her hurt feelings, Bellamy? You're so damn good at it after all," he spits at me.

"It's not my job to clean up after you."

"Could have fooled me. Every time we have a disagreement, she runs straight to you two."

"That's because we actually give a damn about her and her happiness. All you care about is yourself. She is one of the most beautiful, generous, kind, and selfless people on this planet, and she deserves so much more than you, but for some reason, she loves your sorry ass. So, we bite our tongues, and we try to be as happy for her as we can. We don't bad-mouth you or tell her how we truly feel about you. But

I'm done with that shit now. You are a pathetic loser who mistreats her and takes advantage of her generosity and forgiving heart. You use pretty words and hollow promises to manipulate her, and that's over now.

"You have a good woman, Ricky, and you should be kissing the ground she walks on for blessing you with her love. If you can't see that, then hit the road. She'll be fine because we've got her. We have had her, had each other, through every heartbreak, disappointment, and moments of grief for the last twenty years. Men have come and gone in all our lives, but we are a constant and always will be. If you don't like that, tough shit because we aren't going anywhere."

"Whatever. You're a bunch of loudmouth bitches, and you can have each other," he says before he turns on his heel and walks toward the car Sonia bought and paid for.

I lose it. I bolt off the deck and straight for him.

I hear Elle scream for Walker as I dive for his back. The impact of me hurling myself full speed takes him by surprise, and before he can recover, I knee him in his little-boy balls. He drops the keys in his hand as he rolls to his side and howls in pain. I stand and snatch the keys. Then, I look down at him.

"Find yourself a new sugar momma because your free ride is over," I spit at him.

"Give me back my keys, or I'll have your ass arrested for theft and assault, you cunt," he yells.

I laugh in his face. "These keys are to an apartment that belongs to Sonia's mother and a car that is in Sonia's name. You don't have anything worth stealing, and if you want to further curse your manhood, call and report me for tackling you. I'll gladly post the bail for that."

Rage fills his eyes, and he reaches out and grabs my ankle as I move to walk back to the party.

I lose my balance and fall forward face-first into the gravel. He is on my back in an instant, and he wrenches my arm behind me to try and pry the key ring from me. He bends my fingers so far back that I feel my ring finger snap, and pain shoots up my arm, but I hold on to that key ring with everything I have.

"What the fuck!" Walker's voice booms across the parking lot, but Ricky is too stupid or crazy to heed the warning.

He sinks his teeth into my wrist, and I try to throw my elbow back and reach him, but before I can make contact, he is lifted and flying through the air.

"Have you lost your damn mind, son?" Walker asks as he stalks toward Ricky, who shuffles backward, trying to get to his feet.

"Don't kill him, baby. Just break his legs or something. I don't want you having to wear prison orange in our wedding photos," Elle shouts.

Ricky's eyes fly to Walker as he makes it to him. He grabs Ricky by the collar of his shirt and raises him off the ground with one hand.

"Don't you ever lay a hand on a woman again. Especially one of my women." He leans in and gets within an inch of Ricky's face. "None of them. Do you understand what I'm saying to you?"

Ricky doesn't answer.

Walker twists his fist harder in his shirt, and Ricky starts to turn reddish blue.

"I said, do you understand what I'm saying?"

Ricky brings his hands to his throat and pulls on Walker's grip as he nods.

"Good."

He drops him to the ground and turns back to us, leaving him sputtering in the dirt. Walker walks back to me and Elle. He takes the keys from my hand and shoves them into his pocket, and then he inspects my hand.

"Can you bend your fingers?"

I shake my head but don't complain. I won't give that asshole the satisfaction.

"I have electrical tape in my truck. We can tape those fingers together for now," he says as he lightly touches the teeth marks on my wrist.

Elle can tell he is about to turn back for Ricky, so she wraps an arm around his waist.

He looks over at her and smiles a tight smile as he wraps an arm around each of us, hooking our necks.

"Come on now, ladies. There's a cake that needs to be cut and eaten. Y'all are always starting some shit when I'm hungry," he complains as he leads us back into the party.

Forty-One

BELLAMY

I GO TO THE RESTROOM AND CLEAN MYSELF UP AS ELLE CONSOLES Sonia. Once we have ourselves pulled together, we rally for Doreen and rejoin the party. Sophie takes a microphone, and then one by one, people come up to take their turns, saying what Doreen means to them. She sobs the entire time as everyone shares funny memories and times she bestowed wisdom. Walker spends about twenty minutes just praising her cooking. When it's Emmett's turn, he has Braxton cue up a song on the jukebox.

"This says all I need to. Will you dance with me?" he asks.

She stands to join him as "You're the One That I Want" from the *Grease* soundtrack starts to play, and everyone goes nuts.

She turns bright red as he sings to her and spins her around the floor. As the song ends, he gets down on a knee, and she yelps.

"I figure after more than thirty years of courting, it's time I made an honest woman of you," he starts but does not get to finish because she begins blubbering incoherently and buries her face in his neck.

He looks out to the crowd and says, "I heard a yes in there somewhere."

A roar of congratulations rises, and everyone comes at them at once.

The happiness makes Sonia run for the restroom again, and as we walk after her, I feel a hand reach for mine.

I look back to see Brandt standing there.

"I'm heading out. Mr. Lancaster is bringing Mom home. So, just come over and ring the bell whenever you're ready."

I give him a chin lift and try to pull my hand from his. He doesn't release me but rolls my hand over and inspects the bruising that has started to surface.

"What happened?" he asks.

"I got in a fight with Ricky in the parking lot."

He snaps his eyes to mine. "With Ricky?"

"Yep."

He lets me go when I tug away again.

"I'll be by in a bit," I tell him and hurry after my girls.

I find them in the restroom, and Elle is consoling a sobbing Sonia in her arms.

I wrap my arms around them both, and we just hold each other. Elle and I pour our strength into her.

After she cries it all out, she looks at us in the mirror. "I'm sorry that I didn't listen to you guys. You have to think I'm so stupid for loving him."

Elle disengages, and she grabs her face and turns it to her. "I am always going to be here for you. No matter what. I'll be the one driving the getaway car when you need a rescue. I'll be fussing, saying, *This don't make no sense*, and screaming, *What the hell is wrong with you*, and, *Have you lost your damn mind?* But I'll still be driving the car. You got me?"

"I got you," Sonia whispers.

"There is something better out there for you. I promise," Elle assures her.

Sonia shakes her head.

"You got the fairytale with Walker, but I don't think a happily ever after is in the cards for me."

"Of course it is!" I cry. "You're forgetting the most important part of the happily ever after."

"What's that?" Sonia asks, confused.

I throw my arms up, as if it should be obvious, and then explain.

"In order to have a happy ending, you must endure a hellacious middle, silly!"

Sonia starts to giggle through her tears as Elle agrees with me.

"It's true; you're just about to get to the good part of your story."

Sonia finally manages a smile.

"Yeah, maybe. At least I have you guys and that is enough for now."

And that sums up our friendship. Ride or die.

Walker gets Foster to follow us in Sonia's car to her apartment. While Elle gets her settled in, Walker and Foster change her locks out with the ones Walker had in his truck, which he purchased for his and Elle's new home. I walk down the few blocks to Brandt's office.

I know I only worked with him for a couple of weeks, but I miss it. Not just him, but also the clients and the animals.

What a crazy summer it has been. My heart aches at the thought of leaving. Sonia is going to need Elle and me more than ever, Faith just got here, Beau is growing like a weed and will be a little man soon, and Elle will be planning her wedding. I'm going to miss so much of it all if I leave now. Most of all, I'll miss Brandt. I'll miss seeing what the house looks like, painted blue. I'll miss him taking me home and passing me off to my daddy at night. I'll miss his kisses and his arms around me.

How did this happen? How did my heart get so attached to him so quickly when I wasn't paying attention?

I wasn't this upset about ending things with Derrick after knowing him for years? Maybe Doreen is right; God does have a soul mate for us all, and it's not about the length of time you've spent together but about you finding your matching piece.

I'm standing outside, trying to figure out how I'm going to say all of this to him when the light comes on and he opens the door.

My heart skips a beat as I pass him to walk inside. I sit on the edge of the desk and wait as he shuts the door behind me.

When he turns to face me, my stomach drops. I know instantly that this isn't about us talking and figuring out where we stand or how we want to proceed with our relationship.

This is good-bye.

It's written all over him.

Forty-Two

BRANDT

"YOU WANT TO GO TO MY OFFICE?" I ASK AS I TURN TO FACE her.

She shakes her head. "Nope. I think we can say everything that needs to be said right here," she says.

I notice a scratch across her cheek from her nose to ear. I reach out to touch it, and she flinches.

"You really got in a fight with a man in the parking lot tonight?" I ask in disbelief.

"Yep. Don't worry. I didn't hurt him too badly," she says cheekily.

I shake my head. "So reckless," I mumble.

"What did you say?"

"I said, you're reckless, Bellamy. Crazy, wild, beautiful, and completely reckless."

"And that's what, a bad thing? That I love my friends recklessly and would fight the Devil himself for messing with them?"

I sigh. "I didn't say it was a bad thing, but it's something that I can't have in my life."

Her face goes blank at my declaration.

"At least I know why you ghosted me," she says as she crosses her arms over her chest. The blue-and-purple bite mark exposed on her wrist.

A pounding ache bubbles in my chest at the sight. I want to find that asshole and turn his entire body those colors.

"It's not you—" I begin.

She cuts me off, "Do not give me that lame-ass line. Please, at least spare me that humiliation."

"I'm not trying to hurt you or humiliate you, Bellamy," I tell her.

"You know what? I'm going to let you off the hook easy, Doc. Turns out, Denver Zoo wants me after all. I'll start looking for apartments in the city next week. I just wanted to let you know."

"That's wonderful, Bellamy. I know that's what you wanted," I tell her as that ache grows to a pulsing thrum.

"Yep. My dream come true," she declares as she avoids my eyes.

I approach her and reach to hug her. I just want to hold her against me one more time before I let her go.

"Don't," she demands as she throws her hand up between us.

"I don't want to hurt you," I whisper.

"Too late." She walks past me and to the door.

She opens it, but then she stops and turns around. Tears are welling in her eyes.

"I came here tonight to say my piece, dammit, and I'm not going to chicken out now. I get that you have been through some really horrible shit in your life. I hate that you had to endure that. I wish that you had learned a lesson from what you'd lost—that life is precious. The moments you have are all you get, and you should live those to the fullest every single day.

"But you are wasting your second chance. You want to squander it all away, feeling sorry for yourself? Well, be my guest. But let's be clear about something: it's a choice.

"I told myself that you had a fragile heart, which had been shattered, and that getting close to you was a bad idea, but it turns out, I'm the one with the fragile heart, and you're just a coward. If you're going to let the rest of your life be filled with a whole lot of nothing so you never have the chance of experiencing pain again, then you might as well have died that day too. You're going to have nothing but an empty life in a big, lonely house. I bet your Annie would agree with me when I say, that's a waste. Good-bye, Brandt."

She drops her bomb and goes out the door without another backward glance.

I thought I was going to be the one gutting her.

But I felt every single word she said hit my skin like the sear of a hot branding iron.

Forty-Three

BRANDT

"THAT'S THE LAST ONE, MAN," WALKER SAYS AS HE CARRIES the last gallon of paint from the back of the truck. "Where do you want to start? Front or back?"

I stand there, looking up at the house I thought I liked two days ago.

"What are we looking at?" he asks as he follows my line of sight.

"An empty life in a big, lonely house," I repeat her words.

"What?" He turns to me.

"Thanks for your help, Walker, but you don't have to stick around. I don't think I'll be very good company today."

"Is this about Bells taking off?" he asks.

"Yes. No. I didn't know she had left already."

Damn, that was fast.

"Elle took her to the airport last night," he informs.

I nod as I continue to look up at the house. I have no idea what I was thinking, buying it. Maybe I wasn't thinking; I was just hoping.

"She thought this was a dream house," I tell him.

"A dream house, huh? Well, I don't know much, but the one thing I do know is a dream house isn't built with wood, stone or the perfect slab of granite. No, it's created when every corner, crack and crevice is filled with love and laughter. It's built by the memories made by the people within it. This here is just a shell. It's up to you to make it a dream come true."

"I don't think I'm capable," I admit.

"You know, I never intended to do anything with my life but sit in that little shack and drink myself to death. I thought the worst thing that could happen to a man was a broken heart, and I wasn't about to put mine out there to get trampled on ever again. I was wrong though. The worst thing that can happen to a man is to waste his life in a house, drinking himself to death, having a heart and never using it, just letting all the love he has to give someone wither up. Life is for living. Hard work, good friends, delicious food, cold beer. And a good woman by your side, warming your bed, loving you with all of her body and soul, giving you babies, and giving you shit to keep you on your toes. I know it can be scary—the thought of having it and losing it. Especially for you because you know what that feels like better than anyone. But if you never go for it and you let it walk right out of your door and into some other asshole's happily ever after, then you'll lose it anyway," he says as he clasps my shoulder.

"I don't want to hold her back," I tell him.

"Hold her back? Man, we can't hold these women back. They will plow toward their happiness and grab you by the collar and drag you with them. Now, if we ain't doing this today, then I'm going to go scoop my happiness up and take her horseback riding," he says.

"Sounds like fun."

"She loves to ride, and I love to watch her laugh as she does."

He releases his hold on me and heads to his truck.

"Hey, Doc," he calls to me, and I turn.

"My granddaddy used to tell me that there's a battle raging inside every man. Two wolves. One is called regret and anger. The other is called love and hope. You know which one wins?"

"Which one?" I ask.

"The one you feed."

I walk upon the scene once again. Annie is pulling on her coat as she leaves the restaurant in a huff and starts to walk out to the parking lot. My attention snaps to the dumpster on the left, and I brace for what is coming next when, all of a sudden, she stops and looks right at me. Then, she veers off in my direction.

This isn't how it's supposed to go.

She marches up to me and stops. I see annoyance in her eyes.

"What are you doing, Brandy? Why do you keep coming back to this place over and over again and dragging me with you?" she asks, not hiding her frustration.

I take a few tentative steps forward.

"I just come to see you," I tell her.

"But it's not real," she whispers.

I look past her, searching for the man in the dirty, dark jacket. Preparing to hurl myself between them.

"You can't save me, sweetheart. It's not ever going to end differently. You have to stop torturing yourself."

"I don't know how to make it stop. Everything still hurts."

"Yes, you do. You have to stop punishing yourself. I'm not here anymore. I've moved on, and you need to move on too," she says.

"What if I can't?" I choke out.

"You can. You've already started," she informs me as she reaches up and cradles my cheek with her hand. "Where is she?"

"Where's who?" I ask, confused.

"Bellamy, silly," she answers.

"Bellamy? She's gone. She took a job in Denver," I tell her.

"And you just let her go? What are you afraid of?"

I take a deep breath as a pang of regret rises in my throat.

"She's better off without me," I answer honestly.

"She's not me, Brandy. She loves you, and she'll never be better off without you."

"I … I-I'm sorry," I finally say the words I need her to hear. "I'm sorry I wasn't on time that night. I'm sorry he hurt you and that I wasn't there to protect you. Sorry that I let work steal our time."

"It wasn't your fault," she says.

"I wasn't there for you. You left because I had disappointed you again."

"It wasn't your fault," she says again.

"I promised you I'd be there, and I wasn't."

"And it still wasn't your fault."

"I wish I had made it before—"

"Why? We both would have been killed," she interrupts angrily.

I meet her eyes. "Yes, it's what I deserve."

"Stop that. Stop it now. Stop wasting all this time and stop pushing happiness away. Can't you see you're doing the same thing to her that you did to me?"

That gets my attention.

"What?"

"She needs you to show up for her."

"I …" I turn away from her as regret tightens its grip on my throat, and words escape me.

She reaches up and grabs my chin, gently forcing my eyes back to hers. She smiles.

"You fell in love," she murmurs.

"I didn't mean to," I whisper as tears fill my vision, and her face blurs.

"Why are you here?" she asks again.

"I don't want you to have to go through this alone," I admit.

"Oh, sweetheart, the only one who's going through this alone night after night is you," she says.

"I'm afraid, Annie."

"Of what?"

"That, one day, a whole day will go by, and I won't think of you."

"When that day comes—and I pray it does for you—it will be okay. You have to let go of this guilt. You have to let go of me. Don't waste any more precious time. I want you to live," she says.

"I miss you," I confess.

"You'll always have me. My heart is yours forever." She takes her hand from my cheek and places it on my chest. "But it's time to give someone else yours. *Go after her and don't come back to this place anymore. Be happy. That's all I want from you. Live well and be happy."*

She stands on her tiptoes and places a kiss to my chin, like she always used to do.

"Good-bye, sweetheart," I say as I pull her to me and squeeze her tightly. "I hope wherever you are, you are cradled in love," I say into her hair.

I open my eyes, and I'm in my bed. Tears streaming down my cheeks and one thought in my mind.

I have to go get my girl.

Forty-Four

BRANDT

I GET UP, AND MOM COMES OUT OF HER ROOM. WE MEET IN THE hallway.

I kiss her cheek loudly as I pass her on the way to the kitchen.

"Are you okay, son?" she asks as she follows me.

"I will be," I tell her.

I grab my keys and wallet.

She looks at the clock on the stove and asks, "Where are you going at this hour?"

"Denver."

"Denver? You have appointments starting at eight," she reminds me.

Shit.

I turn to face her. "I need you to call and reschedule everything for the next few days."

Her eyes widen. "You're closing the office?" she asks in surprise.

"Yes, move everything to next week. I'll work some night hours and weekends to make up the work."

"And if there is an emergency?" she asks, flustered.

"Send them to the clinic in Aurora. I'll call Greg and tell him what's happening, and he'll see to the emergencies."

"Aurora is over an hour from here," she tells me something I already know.

I stop and look back to her. "Hopefully, nothing urgent comes up, but I have to go. I have to tell Bellamy how I feel. If I don't, I'll regret it for the rest of my life."

Her eyes fill with tears, and she sits at the table.

"Mom?"

I sit beside her, and her hand comes to my cheek.

"I'm proud of you. You've been sleepwalking through your life the last couple of years, and you're finally starting to wake up."

I lean into her touch.

"Go, and don't come back without her."

I kiss her cheek again and then race to Myer's house. It's five in the morning, and he should be up and heading to Stoney Ridge any minute.

I pull up and park. I walk up onto the porch. I can see him inside, walking back and forth in front of the kitchen island.

I knock lightly and wait.

He opens the door, carrying his baby girl, who is bundled up in a fuzzy blanket. The smile on his face is replaced with a scowl.

"Awfully early for a visit, isn't it, Doc?"

"Yeah, sorry about the time, but I need to know where Bellamy is."

He leans against the doorframe. "And why would you need to know that?"

I swallow hard, and then I look him in the eye. "Because I love her and I need to tell her that."

I can tell that was not the answer he'd expected.

"You love her?"

"More than anything, and I know that it might be too late, but if I don't tell her, I'm afraid that I'm going to sit in the shack and drink myself to death."

"Come again?" he asks, confused by my babbling.

"I just need to know where to find her. This isn't something I can say to her over the phone. Please," I beg.

A head of red curls looks around him and grins.

"Hyatt Regency, downtown Denver," she says before reaching up and taking the baby from Myer and walking back inside.

"Hyatt Regency," I repeat to myself as I turn back to my truck to get my phone.

"Doc?" Myer calls after me, and I stop and turn back to face him. "Only an insane man would take advice from Walker Reid."

"That's me, as crazy as they come."

He laughs.

"By the way, you'll be getting a call from my mom to reschedule your castration appointment. I'm taking a couple of days off. Family emergency."

"Go get Bells and bring her home. And if you aren't successful, I wouldn't eat or drink anything my mother offers you when you come to the ranch going forward, if you know what I'm saying."

He gives me a salute and shuts his door.

I dial the Hyatt and make a reservation, and then I get on the road.

I'm so anxious to see her that I make it to Denver in record time.

I told myself the entire drive that if she and the ex-boyfriend were trying to work things out, then I would walk away. Let her have the job and the new start without my interference.

But then I decided that asshole had his chance, and I was taking mine.

I check into my room and then head down to the bar. This hotel is a conference center, and it is huge. She could be anywhere.

I sit down and order a drink, and then I people-watch for over an hour. Every time I see someone with long blonde hair walk by, my heart stops.

I finally have had enough of waiting and walk to the reservation desk.

I stand in line, trying to come up with a reasonable explanation for why I need her hotel room number while I wait my turn.

That's when it happens.

I catch a glimpse of her out of the corner of my eye. She heads for the elevator, chatting with another woman. I race to get there before she gets on, but I'm seconds too late. I stand and watch the elevator climb. I make note of the floors that it stops on. Three. It stops on three different floors.

This is where you prove how serious you are, Haralson.

I start at the eighth floor, and I knock on every single door. None of them are hers.

I board the elevator again, and this time, I go to the eleventh floor. I knock on twelve unsuccessful doors before I find her.

The thirteenth door opens, and she is standing there. She has showered and changed since I spotted her downstairs in the navy pantsuit.

Her hair is damp, and she has on lounge shorts and a tank.

Stunning.

She gasps when she sees me. "What are you doing here, Brandt?"

"I came for you."

Her forehead wrinkles in confusion, and I have to fight the urge to kiss those lines away.

Once she's processed my declaration, she frowns.

"Nothing's changed," she says.

"Everything has changed."

Forty-Five

BRANDT

SHE PROTECTIVELY CROSSES HER ARMS OVER HER CHEST. "WHAT do you want from me?"

"You got to say your piece the other night, but there is more I want to say," I start.

"You came all the way here to finish your Dear John speech? Really, Doc?"

"Five minutes. That's all I'm asking for," I beg.

She stands there, debating with herself.

"I'll sleep here in this hallway if I have to, Bellamy."

She raises an eyebrow and looks at me like she would love nothing more than for me to sleep on the cold, hard, filthy floor.

"I will."

I'm a man with nothing to lose.

"Fine," she huffs. "Five minutes, and I'm timing you."

She turns and walks back into her room, leaving the door open for me to follow.

She sits on the end of the bed and clicks the television off.

Her expectant eyes look up at me, and she waits.

I take a deep breath and let it all out. "I was a prisoner when we met. Locked up in a cell of grief. I don't know how I ended up there, but I couldn't get myself out. It got comfortable in that cell. So much so that I didn't even realize I was there. Until you came along. It was you. Falling in love was the key that unlocked the prison door. You set me free, Bellamy Wilson."

Her eyes fill with tears. "You love me?"

"I do," I whisper.

"How do you know? What changed in a couple of days?"

"I know I'm in love with you because, for the first time in a long time, I'd rather be awake than asleep. Because happiness is here with you and not held hostage in my dreams anymore. I didn't think it was possible to feel anything so powerful again."

I take a tentative step forward.

"I know you have your own dreams, and I know this job is important to you. And I support anything that makes you happy. So, if here is where you need to be right now, we'll work it out. I'll drive up every weekend. I'll find a job and relocate to be closer to you."

"What about the house?" she asks.

"It can sit there and rot again for all I care."

Her mouth falls open.

"Or I'll sell it. Or Mom can live there, and we can visit. I don't care."

"Don't you dare sell the dream house," she says.

"Your dream house?" I ask.

"Our dream house."

"Do you love me?" I ask her.

"I turned the job down."

"Then, why are you in Denver?" I ask her, confused.

"I was checking out the vet tech program at Bel-Rea. One of my professors from Chicago is teaching there now."

"You want to be a vet tech?"

She shrugs. "It's a woman's prerogative to change her mind."

"There's a big demand for techs. I can put a good word in for you in the industry," I tell her.

She grins. "Much obliged."

"Do you love me?" I ask her again.

She nods.

That does it.

I walk toward her, and she throws herself in my arms. I've never felt relief like I do at this moment.

"Say it again," she demands softly.

I'll say it as many times as she needs me to.

"I love you. I love your hair. I love your teeth. I love that freckle behind your right ear. I love the scar on your hip. I love everything about you, Bellamy."

I drop my forehead to hers.

"Come back. Build a practice, a home, a family … build a life with me. Please."

"Okay."

I find her mouth with mine, and I kiss her like a starved man as I back her up to the bed.

I lay her down and bear up to look at her. She grabs my hair and pulls me back to her mouth. Then, she wraps her legs around my hips and holds me in place.

I chuckle.

"I just want to look at you, baby," I whisper against her lips.

She doesn't let me up. She nips at my mouth and bites my bottom lip.

"I just want to feel you," she utters as she slides her hands down the front of my shirt and tugs it loose from my jeans, so she can get to my skin.

I let her explore. She can have whatever she wants.

Her fingertips graze my chest and down my rib cage. She stops at the top of my jeans.

"I want to taste you," she says as she pushes me to my back. Then, she kisses the space below my belly button as her hands work the button of my jeans.

I take her hair and twist it into my hand, so I can lift it and see her face.

She arches up and pulls the tank up, and I move my hands to help her slide it over her head. Her hair falls down over her bare breasts. I bring my hand to the side of her neck, and her eyes flutter to mine.

"You are exquisite, baby."

She runs her nails over the hem of my boxers and into the top of my pants.

I grow painfully hard at the contact, and I groan, fighting the urge to take over.

Her slow perusal drives me mad as my body coils tight.

"Are you trying to torture me?" I ask.

She brings her mouth to my ear and whispers, "Maybe." Then, she sucks my earlobe into her mouth and bites down.

My hips buck up off the bed, and she starts to giggle.

Tease.

I feed my hands into the back of her shorts and slide my finger between her legs. She gasps and arches her back.

She comes up to her knees and grabs the sides of my jeans. I lift my hips, and she yanks them down my thighs. My erection springs free, and she runs a nail over the head. I twitch with anticipation as she firmly wraps her hand around me. Finally, she dips her hot, sweet mouth to circle the tip with her tongue as her hand moves up and down. I fist my hand in her hair and start to massage her scalp as she shallows me deep.

She takes her time, savoring my cock. When I feel myself getting close to losing control, I halt her.

She whimpers as I slide from her lips.

"I want to be inside you when I come."

She kicks her shorts off, and I flip her onto her back. Her legs fall open, and her glistening core invites me to claim her. I climb her body, and I place a kiss to her lips as I push inside.

She arches her back and offers her chest to my mouth as she starts to move her hips to meet my thrusts.

I lean back and watch her face as her breath grows ragged and her eyes roll back. I grow thicker inside her, and I bring my mouth to her breast, take a taut nipple between my lips, and suck it gently.

Her hand flies to my shoulder and I feel the sharp tip of her fingernails dig in to my flesh as a tremor runs the length of her body.

She moans my name, and it is the sweetest sound I have ever heard. I increase my pace, and her legs start to tremble as I circle her clit with my thumb. She cries out, and I take her mouth and swallow every gasp and moan as I love her. I try to hold on, but I'm too far gone. She raises her hips to drive me deeper and deeper inside.

My release rockets down my spine and into her. She wraps her arms around my neck and bites down hard into the meat of my shoulder as she comes hard.

I continue to ease in and out of her until her body stops quaking and she goes limp in my arms.

I tuck her into my side and pull the sheet over us.

"Say it again," she murmurs without opening her eyes.

"I love you."

She smiles a sleepy smile.

"I love you more than doughnuts."

I bark out a laugh and she grins as her heavy eyelids fall shut.

I watch as she drifts off to sleep.

Then, I follow her into sweet dreams.

Epilogue

BRANDT
Six Months Later

"ARE YOU READY? WE STILL HAVE TO GO PICK MOM UP," I call up the stairs.

"I'm coming," Bellamy announces as she hurries down the steps in a form-fitting black dress, her heels dangling from her fingertips.

I walk over and take the heels from her. I bend to help her get them on as she uses the banister to balance herself.

"It's your fault I'm running so late," she says as she steps into one shoe.

I glide my hand up to caress her calf as she picks the other foot up.

"My fault?"

"Yes, your fault. If you had not joined me in the shower, I would have been ready an hour ago," she accuses.

I look up at her, and her eyes heat as she remembers why I interrupted her.

I slip her other shoe on, and I move my hand from her calf up to the inside of her thigh.

"Don't," she warns as I reach the edge of her silk panties. "We're already late, remember? And it's our event."

I drop my hand, and she lets out a mewl of protest.

I raise an eyebrow at her, and she pushes my face from her and slides past me to the table at the door, where she picks up her clutch.

Today, we are launching the new nonprofit called Annie's Heart. The charity will aid in matching older children in the foster care system with families who have been counseled to handle the issues particular to children who lost their parents or guardians between the ages of ten and eighteen. It will also help to pay for the continued education of the child when they graduate high school and age out of the system. It was Bellamy's brainchild. She said it was a way to honor Annie and keep her memory alive.

We make our way to pick Mom up at the apartment above my clinic that she and I used to share. When the house was finished and move-in ready, she sat me down and explained that she wanted a place to call her own and that she enjoyed living downtown and being able to walk to the shops and restaurants. She wanted independence and she wanted Bellamy and me to have a place to all our own. Bellamy splits her time between here and her apartment in Denver. She attends classes four days a week and spends her weekends here with me, until she finishes tech school and can finally come home to me and our practice.

It's funny, I had thought that I was taking care of Mom at this point in her life, but it would seem that the only reason she was living under my roof was to take care of me, and now, my well-being is no longer something that worries her.

I take Bellamy's hand in mine and kiss the finger that wears my ring.

As of about two hours ago, I decided I could wait no longer, and I got into the shower with her and slid it on her hand while her head was under the spray and her eyes were closed. She opened them and looked down at the diamond. Immediately, she burst into tears, and rather than say yes, she backed me up against the wall of the shower and answered me with her mouth in another way. The whole thing finished with us tangled in damp sheets and running late.

Beverly is going to be pissed when we arrive and she sees the ring on Bellamy's hand. She wanted to plan some elaborate engagement that involved the ring in a cupcake or something like that, but when I walked in from working in the garden to find Bellamy in the shower, I just knew it was time.

I never thought life could be this beautiful again.

I thank God every day that he sent me to Poplar Falls.

The End

Acknowledgments

First, I want to thank every single reader, blogger, and fellow author who took a chance on this series. What an unexpected and wonderful ride it has been. Poplar Falls and the people that inhabit it, although fictional, have earned a place in my heart. I wish I could pack a bag and board a plane to Colorado and meet up with the girls for a weekend.

Amanda White and Gloria Green, as always, thank you for your encouragement and honest feedback. No matter when I send you my jumbled manuscript you two aways stop what you are doing and help me sort through the chaos in my mind. I love you both.

Autumn Gantz, you are an amazing and hard-working publicist. I honestly couldn't do this author life without you. You go above and beyond for me and all your clients. I can't thank you enough. Ever. Most important, you are an incredible friend. "&" Forever.

Jovana Shirley, what can I say? You are the bomb. Thank you for making me look good. If the world saw the hot-mess first draft of these books, they would know how true that statement is. You are an angel, and commas will always be the devil.

Judy Zweifel, Stacey Blake, Sommer Stein, and Michaela Mangum, thank you for your contributions to this book. You are all incredible at what you do, and I'm truly blessed to have you all be a part of my team.

Last but not least, David Miller, you are the unicorn husband. I couldn't love you more if you were a rancher in Colorado. Fact. The End.

Other Books

Cross My Heart Duet

Both of Me

Both of Us

Poplar Falls

Rustic Hearts

Stone Hearts

Wicked Hearts

Fragile Hearts

About the Author

Amber Kelly is a romance author that calls North Carolina home. She has been a avid reader from a young age and you could always find her with her nose in a book completely enthralled in an adventure. With the support of her husband and family, in 2018, she decided to finally give a voice to the stories in her head and her debut novel, Both of Me was born. You can connect with Amber on Facebook at facebook.com/AuthorAmberKelly, on IG @authoramberkelly, on twitter @AuthorAmberKel1 or via her website www.authoramberkelly.com.

Made in the USA
Monee, IL
21 August 2022